Tales from Cushman Row

A COMPENDIUM OF LOVE

SUANNE LAQUEUR

MJ—

Namoronste ♡

Suanne Lago

INTRODUCTION

THESE ARE SCENES AND SCRIBBLES either cut from the final draft of *A Charm of Finches*, or written with no intent of ever being in the final draft. They were just written.

There is no arc or chronology to this collection. It's not a story and not supposed to be. The scenes will contradict each other. Sometimes they'll repeat. A lot of it is going straight from the notebook to the page here. It's my weird head and The Thing.

There's a lot of sex in here. In fact, it's mostly sex. Frankly, friends, full disclosure and trigger warning: this is a fuckfest. It gets pretty raw and not that you need my advice, but I wouldn't plow through it in one sitting. If you do, I suggest you have a good cleansing read lined up afterward. Like Nietzsche.

Writing all this sex served a certain purpose. Two purposes.

Purpose One: When I started to write *Finches*, before the character of Geno was created, I wanted to get Jav laid. *Spectacularly* laid. He deserved it. It was time to let him figure out who he was, emotionally and sexually. And I wanted to see what kind of game this new guy Steffen Finch had. Was he the transitional person or was he The One? And furthermore (I start too many sentences with 'and'), could I write honest and believable gay sex?

So I poured a glass of wine and opened a new word doc. Cracked my knuckles, cleared my throat and ventured in. *Don't think about it being two men*, I thought. *Think about it being two humans. It's not gay sex, it's just sex. This is Jav. You know Jav better than anyone else on earth. Whatever Stef turns out to be, just make him good for Jav at this point in time. Tell the story.*

For the next two months, I drank and told the story. Stories. Yeah, I could write this. In fact, I couldn't stop writing it. It was time to get on with the book, but...

"These two won't stop screwing," I complained to my friend Camille. "I'm literally drinking wine and writing them in bed every goddamn day. It's like my new hobby."

Writing Jav and Stef fooling around, messing around, screwing, shtupping, carrying on and making love was a piece of layer cake. It was ten kinds of fun. It got kind of worrisome. Was there going to be an eventual book or was it going to be just a boozy fuck-ton of gratuitous boning?

In hindsight, I can say that all this fooling around, used or not, was necessary to not only establish Jav and Stef's relationship, but to give me a solid foundation to stand on. I needed the passionate tenacity of their love to fall back on as I started researching for Geno's story.

Which brings me to Purpose Two.

There's always a post-partum collapse after a book is released. After five books, I expected it. I knew it was coming. But after *Finches*, I was a wreck. After putting this challenging and important story into the world, I was completely, totally, utterly wiped out and exhausted and drained. The tank so empty, it didn't even have fumes. Elizabeth Gilbert says the only thing to do after a triumph or a flop is to go back "home," wherever it may be. So I did. I went back to where *Finches* started, and I wrote Jav and Stef scenes until I felt better. Their love grounded me again. Brought me back to center. Brought me home.

Which is the most important job I have.

–SLQR
November 14, 2017
Somers, New York

TALES FROM CUSHMAN ROW

GOD'S SISTER

Typical. I busted my butt on this NPR transcript and then ended up cutting it from the final draft of *Finches*. I know I've said this before but poor Camberley Jones. I have the best intentions of making her a lead character, but in the end, it's only her voice I need. But it's the kind of voice that builds an empire. —SLQR

"TELL ME A STORY"

TRANSCRIPT FROM THE NATIONAL PUBLIC RADIO SERIES, *MOMENTS IN TIME*

KAREN STARK: YOU'RE LISTENING TO *Moments in Time*. I'm Karen Stark, thanks for joining us.

Author Gil Rafael is best-known for the short story "Bald," which was made into the critically-acclaimed movie in 2004, starring Kristin Scott Thomas. He's since published a collection of short stories and a novella, as well as being a regular contributor to *GQ, Esquire* and the *New Yorker*. His first full-length novel is being released this September. It's called *The Trade* and tells the story of a young woman who works in the World Trade Center on the eve of 9/11. While the terrorist attacks make a tragic end for thousands, it allows this one woman an opportunity to escape her abusive marriage and create a new life.

Producer Camberley Jones met up with Gil Rafael on his home turf of Manhattan, where he's working on his next book. Or rather, he *was* working on his next book, but the research has taken him on an interesting and personal journey.

[Sound: Exterior, street scene, cars, voices]

Camberley Jones: Author Gil Rafael is doing field research in the Latino neighborhoods of New York City. He's collecting stories. Latin American folktales. Rather than read them, he wants to listen to them, straight from the elders of these ethnic enclaves.

Today he's in Sunset Park in Brooklyn, which has one of the highest concentrations of Mexican immigrants in the city. He's made no appointments nor scheduled meetings. He simply walks the neighborhood streets, looking for oral traditions on the stoops and corners.

Gil Rafael: It used to be that wakes were principal occasions for storytelling. When extended family gathered to mourn and you sat up with the dearly departed. When their grief took a rest, people would tell stories. Other times these tales would be told after dinner or at the market. Or during work breaks on large plantations.

So I come to these neighborhoods looking out for the senior immigrants. People who would remember these storytelling occasions. The abuelos and abuelas on the steps or the porches. I just start walking and start looking. I always find someone and I'm always touched by how willing they are to talk to me.

Jones: Gil approaches a silver-haired lady sitting on a stoop of a duplex on 47th Street.

Rafael: Buenas dias, señora

2

Unidentified woman: Buenas dias, niño.

Rafael: Me llamo Javier...

Jones: Gil Rafael is a pen name. He introduces himself with his real name, Javier Rafael Gil deSoto. He's first-generation Dominican-American, his parents immigrated in the early sixties. He grew up in the Corona section of Queens before moving to the larger, established Dominican neighborhood of Inwood, at the tip of Manhattan.

The woman's name is Inez and she's eighty-four. After she was widowed in 1990, she came to the states from Mexico to live with her daughter. Gil asks if she knows any stories. Folktales or legends from her childhood.

Rafael: ¿Conocen alguna historias?

Inez: ¿De historias, niño? ¿Qué tipo de historias?

Rafael: Un cuento popular. Una vieja leyenda. De tu infancia.

Inez: Oh, sí, sí, sí. Por supuesto. Siéntate, querido.

Jones: She invites Gil to sit on the stoop, noble as a queen granting an audience. Other family members come out to listen as well. Her tale starts out as a well-known Christmas story, but then takes a surprising turn.

Inez (In Spanish): When Jesus was born, three kings came to visit him and adore him. One was an American, the other was a Mexican, the last was an Indian.

When they arrived, all three knelt and worshipped the child, then each gave a present. The American king gave money. The Mexican king gave Jesus some swaddling clothes. And the Indian king, who was very poor, had nothing to give, so he danced before Jesus.

Jesus told them he would grant each a gift and asked what they wanted.

The American king said he wanted to be smart and have power. And Jesus granted his wish. For that reason Americans are powerful.

The Mexican King said he wished to believe in the saints and pray. And for that reason Mexicans believe in the saints and pray.

Then Jesus asked the Indian king what he wanted, and the Indian king said he was very poor and humble and would take whatever Jesus would give. So Jesus gave him seeds of corn and wheat and melons and other fruits. And that's why Indians have to work always to live.

[Laughter, spoken Spanish]

Rafael: You can see how Latino folklore blends Old World and New World. Medieval and ancient story types that came with the Spanish conquest were re-framed within Native American narratives. The result was a new mixed lore of European and native heritage. All these new tales are heavy with religious imagery and influence. You'll hear God and the Virgin and saints and angels mixed up with more native or pagan sounding characters.

Jones: A middle-aged man called Mariano speaks up.

Mariano: When I was a young kid, my grandmother and my aunts told a story. A creation story, like Genesis. But it had one part that always bothered me. So the story goes like this:

"The true God took up one ounce of earth and began to work it.

'What are you doing?' asked God's sister.

God answered, 'Something you might not know more about than I.'"

And I'd stop my grandmother right there, saying "Wait, abuela. Wait, wait. God's sister? God has a sister?"

[Laughter]

Mariano: I couldn't let it go. "What do you mean, God's sister? That's not in the bible. Who is she? What happened to her? Where did she go?"

Rafael: What did they say?

Mariano: They wouldn't tell me. "Never mind, never mind, it's not important, it's just an expression." But I minded. You know? If God had a sister, well... That must have come from somewhere, right? It must've been a native influence or something. A sneaky way to remember an old goddess.

Jones: Gil Rafael's been collecting stories for weeks now and plans to write a compilation of Latino folklore.

Rafael: I didn't choose this project, it kind of chose me. I was starting to write a fantasy-adventure story I'd been kicking around for about five years. I had a bunch of characters in my head and a bare bones plot. Then I realized I had to build a world for them to exist in. And a world needs gods. Or goddesses. It needs its legends and myths and heroes and villains. So I started researching mythical archetypes and it got me wondering about my own heritage. I didn't know any Dominican folktales. Or at least, if I'd even been told them, I'd forgotten.

So I like to eat breakfast at this one restaurant up in Inwood. Big Dominican neighborhood. I've been eating there for years and they know me pretty well. The owner's mother is there sometimes, she's in her late seventies, maybe. One day I tell her what I'm doing and ask if she knows any Dominican legends or old stories. Her eyes light up and she laughs, and she tells me about Don Dinero and Doña Fortuna. Mr. Money and Mrs. Fortune, arguing about who was more important.

What struck me, besides it being a good story, was the effect the telling had on some of the other patrons in the restaurant. Like the place got hushed and people turned in their chairs and booths to listen. A lot of them nodding, like they knew the story. *Oh yes. This is true.* And at the end, some of them recited the last line as if it were a response to a prayer in church, "Without good fortune, money is nothing."

All at once I had this fire in my belly to hear more. But I didn't want to read them, I wanted to hear them. Listen to them being told in their natural habitat, so to speak.

That's the funny thing about being a writer. Or any kind of artist, I guess. Sometimes an idea comes to you and it patiently waits its turn. Other times, it's like a cat lying across your keyboard, demanding attention right now or it will make your life hell. I've learned not to fight with the muse. I never win. So I closed up the adventure story and started hitting the streets. It seems to be what I'm supposed to be doing because it's opening up gates in my mind and giving me a lot of other ideas.

It's also satisfying in a soulful kind of way. It's giving my heritage back to me. I left home when I was seventeen and became estranged from my people. My parents are both gone now, and my sister as well. I just have one nephew. Him and I are the last Gil deSotos. He knows less than I do about these legends, so it's not only interesting work to me, it feels like important work as well. It means something.

Jones: I spent four days following Gil Rafael from neighborhood to neighborhood. Jackson Heights, which is home to Argentineans, Columbians and Uruguayans. Corona, which has moved from being a Dominican neighborhood to a largely Ecuadorian one. From the Salvadorian enclave in Flushing to the Hondurans in the Bronx, to the Puerto Ricans in Bushwick, Spanish Harlem and Loisaida, Gil finds the abuelas and asks...

Rafael: ¿Cuéntame una historia?

Jones: Sometimes he takes notes. Mostly he sits and listens.

Rafael: It's more polite. But also, I like to take in the whole story and then see what sticks in my head. Usually whatever lingers around in my mind is the thing I want. Then I have to quick write it down or it will dance off looking for another storyteller. I hate when that happens.

Jones: Gil takes out his notebook, its pages filled with scribblings.

Rafael: This book is my life. Okay, so here's a thing that stayed with me after hearing some of the Mexican stories. "One day a poor man who had no ears, no thumbs and no big toes." I could totally make a character from that. Oh, and this. "It was the chocolate hour." I mean, that's one you hear twice. First time, oh. Second time, *oh.*

Jones: The chocolate hour.

Rafael: Wouldn't that be a great book title? Anyway, I noticed how nearly all legends and tales begin with the word "once." As if it never happened before the telling or since. A lot of the stories end with death or a wedding. Problems are solved quickly and justice is swift and immediate. *He killed the man and all was well.*

Jones: And then it was the chocolate hour.

Rafael (laughing): Exactly. Funny, but a lot of times, the unlikable guy ends up winning. The tales don't always leave you satisfied. They're often unfair. But always they have a little saying at the end, like a curtain call for the teller. They're all so similar, I started writing them down. Here. Mexico: "This tale will last if it's true. If it's just a tale, it's through."

Bolivia: "That's the story. There's no more."

Costa Rica: "And I? I went in one end and came out the other so you, my friends, could tell me another."

Panama: "My tale goes only to here. It ends, and the wind carries it off."

Chile: "Here ends my story, and the wind carries it out to sea."

Now here's something you hear both at the beginning and end of Latin American stories: "Listen and learn it, learn to tell it, and tell it to teach it." I love that. It just beautifully describes the work I'm doing right now. Listen to learn. Learn to tell. Tell to teach.

Jones: Gil Rafael's novel *The Trade* comes out in September and you can read an excerpt on our website, along with another Latin American folktale he collected from the immigrant neighborhoods.

For *Moments in Time*, this is Camberley Jones in New York City.

THE MINDFUL HORNDOG

From reading my books, you may have figured out I don't really like to write about conflict within a relationship. I like to write about strong, loving relationships in the face of conflict.

So Jav and Stef had this adorable meeting in Guelisten. I wrote the drive back to New York and it was easy and fun, the chemistry was great. Excellent. Everything is going to plan.

The Thing looked up from filing its nails. *You should throw a wrench in it.*

"Now?" I said.

Mm. The same night. Catch Stef in an awkward situation easily misunderstood.

"Do I have to? Hasn't Jav suffered enough?"

Write it. You don't have to marry it.

Sometimes The Thing is such a yenta. But she's often right, so I scribbled this down in my notebook.

Obviously I didn't marry it. —SLQR

STEF GETS A TEXT from Thomas who's something of a fuck buddy. The buzz of meeting Jav is still crackling in his veins and Stef is suddenly hesitant at diluting it with Thoma-drama. But Tom is persistent so Stef meets him at a local pub for a few drinks. Maybe some other buddies show up. It's a good time but Stef catches himself watching the door, as if Jav is due to show up as well. Reaching for his phone a half-dozen times, wanting to text. Wanting to make sure Jav hasn't texted and Stef couldn't hear the chime.

Christ, who is this guy?

The euphoric buzz gives way to an itchy, frustrated and fretful burn. He hasn't been laid in quite a while. He was sort of getting into the celibacy. The Zen of delaying gratification. Exploring unsatisfied desire. The mindful horndog.

Now he's hungry.

Thirsty.

"Want to split?" Thomas says, sliding a hand down Stef's spine, into a back pocket and squeezing.

They stumble, laughing and carrying on, to Stef's place. They're cracking up on the front steps, Stef trying to get his keys out of his pocket and the key in the lock while Thomas holds him from behind, face buried in Stef's neck. Thomas's laugh breaks off in the middle and he twists away from Stef.

"Can I help you?" he says.

Stef looks up and his stomach plummets to his shoes. Jav is standing on the sidewalk, hands in the pockets of a leather jacket. Dark and beautiful. A narrow-eyed gaze and one corner of his lip smiling.

Oh. Fuck.

"Hey," Stef says, running a hand through his hair and squirming in Thomas' suddenly possessive grip. "Where are you... What are you doing here?"

"Eh. Just walking around being stupid." There is nothing shy or uncertain in his demeanor right now. He could be a close relation of the Jav that Stef met this afternoon.

"I just got back," Stef says, stupidly.

"I see." Jav's in perfect command of the situation and investing zero emotion in it. "Have a good night, you guys," he says, wrapping the casual words around him like a scarf and tossing the end over his shoulder.

"Wait," Stef says softly. A word bubble in the air over his head. A

10

sick feeling in his bones.

Fuck.

"Who was that?" Thomas says.

"He's... Just someone I met."

"Oh. He live around here?"

"No. I mean I don't know."

"Huh." Thomas glances down the street and back. "I get the terrible feeling I've interrupted something."

"No, it's just..." Stef licks his lips and lets the cool night air fill his mouth. All his horned-up lust snuffs out like a candle flame, smothering his chest with smoke.

"Dude, I'm losing my erection here."

A stab of annoyance behind Stef's eyes. "Sorry. Why don't you go home, okay?"

"You fucking kidding me?"

Stef meets his eyes dead-on. "No. Goodnight. Safe home."

Inside the garden apartment, he paces for ten minutes before grabbing his phone and texting Jav: *I'm sorry. That wasn't what it looked like.*

He paces. Finally a text comes back.

Nothing to be sorry about.

I was just drunk and being stupid.

Why are you explaining yourself?

I'm not sure. But I feel like crap now.

Why?

Because I had a good time meeting you today and I wish I'd just gone to bed.

With me?

Stef gives a bark of out-loud laughter, the heat flooding his face. *No. I mean... No. Shut up. LOL.*

I had a good time too.

I was kind of looking for you all night. You know. Like watching the door. Like you were going to show up.

LOL. I guess I picked the wrong door.

And I picked the wrong date.

Stef's filled with equal parts relief and goofiness. He goes around checking windows, turning off lights and turning locks. Brushing his teeth, stripping down to shorts and waiting for the phone to chime.

Jav texts: *Where is he?*

Headed home.

Sorry I killed the mood.

I'm not. Sounds weird, but thanks.

Glad I could help.

Stef falls back onto the bed, holding the phone over his face. *What are you doing tomorrow?*

The reply takes forever.

I don't know. You got a date I could interrupt?

THE BOTTOM

BOSTON.

Jav's last stop on the tour.

Two in the morning and he and Stef were still talking. More than a little drunk and playing Truth or Truth.

"Have you ever had sex without money being involved?" Stef asked.

"Yeah. I didn't get into the business until I was twenty-one so I went to a few rodeos."

"I bet. But no girlfriend."

"No. I was living in one room in Washington Heights. My bank account was a coffee can. Outside of my looks, I wasn't what you'd call a catch."

"Since leaving the business, have you had payment-less sex?"

"Yes."

"And?"

"I told you. I was bored."

"Ah. You did. Your turn."

"You ever get harassed?" Jav said. "I mean, walking down the street with a boyfriend?"

"I've never walked down the street with a boyfriend."

"Would you say you've ever made love with a guy?"

"No."

"No hesitation there."

"It might've been my Y chromosome talking shit. Let me think."

"I can't say I've made love with anyone so..."

"Well, I remember this one time with Quinn," Stef said. "That guy from college who had all my firsts. We were doing it and... Shit, it's hard to put this into words."

"You don't have to."

"No, I want to, but I'm kind of drunk."

"I'm drunk, too. And I don't offend easy. Say whatever."

"You know what I hate?"

"What?"

"When it comes to male-on-male, you got no good words. Pussy may be crude but it's still got sex appeal. You go to bed with a guy and you got crack. Ass crack. Ass cheeks. Asshole. *Anus.*"

Jav's laugh bounced off the hotel room walls.

"No sexy terminology whatsoever," Stef said. "Anyway, what was I saying?"

"Crack, cheeks and this one time with Quinn?"

"Oh. Yeah. So comes this one night we're doing it."

"It?"

"It."

"Top or bottom?"

"With him I bottomed. He had no interest otherwise."

"Huh." Jav rearranged a few mental pictures. He always pictured Stef topping.

"Up until then," Stef said, "he'd always been behind me. And hell, I didn't know any different, I figured that's how it went. Fuck, I'm drunk. So this one night we're doing it and he's on top of me. I mean, I'm on my back and he's...on me."

"Missionary."

"Yeah. And call me naïve or stupid or whatever, but I didn't know you could do it like that. It threw me a little, because..." He trailed off a few seconds. "The idea is there. It just doesn't want to turn into words. Give me a minute."

"Take your time."

"I was under him," Stef said. "I got my arms and legs up around his body. I'm just spread out for him and I have this really clear thought, *This is what a girl does.* It's like an instinctive...classification. I'm in the submissive role. The bottom. The captive."

"The bitch in the scenario."

14

"Right. The one not in control. Because I'm opening up, you know? I'm opening up so he can get in me. I'm an entrance and not the force. And everything in my mind points to it and says, *feminine*. I never had that kind of thought when he was behind me, but now I'm face-to-face and looking up at him. Holding his eyes. Putting my knees and arms up around him. Does this make sense?"

It did, in that Jav could picture the action. But when he put himself in Stef's place, it didn't make sense. Nor was it anything he found sexy. Putting himself in Quinn's position, however...

"You there?" Stef said.

Jav nodded, transfixed, before remembering Stef couldn't see him. "Still here," he said. "I get it."

"Then the thought of it as a feminine behavior is followed by this insane flash of insight that I'm wrong. Everything I thought about being a man and sex and masculinity... Right at the moment, it all turns inside-out and *right* side out. Like I'd been living backward up until that point. It's not a matter of gender. It's not about positions or power. Entrance or force or top or bottom. Who puts it in and who takes it in. And I relaxed into it. Let it be part of the leaning thing I talked about the other night. I looked up at him and he looked down at me and the eye contact definitely took it to another level. Came my fucking brains out."

"Good evening, and thank you."

"I don't know if I'd call it making love, but it was a bit more than just fucking."

"What made you guys break up?"

Stef snorted. "He dumped me for some chick who gave better blow jobs."

"Did he actually say that?"

"Yeah. Hurt my feels."

They laughed, but it trickled away into an awkward silence.

"What was that like for you?" Stef said.

"What?"

"Getting paid to be blown."

Now Jav snorted. "It didn't happen too often."

"No?"

"It was rarely about me."

"Ah. You were giving more than getting."

"Yeah. Usually I was on the receiving end because the woman wanted to role-play some alpha male scenario where I ordered her around."

"You'd do that?"

"If she paid, I played."

"Huh."

"But I was never, like, lying back and getting it because we were in love and she wanted to please me."

A beat. "This is a weird question, but when was the last time you lay back and had it be all about you?"

"I don't remember." He closed his eyes. Thinking, hoping, *Maybe you and I could...do something about that.*

"I see," Stef said. Soft in Jav's ear. The same thoughtful, hopeful tone in his voice whispering, *Yeah. Maybe we could.*

SMUG

A SMILE LIFTED UP JAV'S mouth, making every hair on Stef's body lift up. God, that mouth. His mouth and his body under his clothes. The skin that stretched over muscle and bone. The frame enclosing all that vulnerability. Stef wanted to touch him. Move up and put his head on Jav's shoulder. Instead he pivoted sideways on the bed, and rested the back of his head against Jav's hip, pillowed against his side. He folded his hands on his chest, knees crossed, one socked foot jiggling. This was good. Bodily contact without the intense scrutiny of eye contact.

"Honestly," Stef said. "There's a world of stuff to do before topping or bottoming comes into the picture. And if it never comes in, so what? It's not the gold standard. For what it's worth, I like it, but it's not my automatic go-to."

His head rose and fell as Jav took a deep breath. "I just wondered if this was all kind of frustrating to you."

"Physically frustrating?"

"Or mentally."

"Mentally, no. Frustrating isn't the word."

"What is it then?"

"Interesting," Stef said. "It's new. I've never done this." He waved a general hand at the two of them and the room. "Lie around with a guy talking about sex. Lie around fully dressed shooting the shit with no expectation. Yeah, I get impatient and physically worked up over you. I'm a mortal male. Sex is always lurking around in my head, usually right behind food. But I'm also forty years old. I can deal with delayed gratification. It's kind of cool, actually."

"For real?"

He closed his eyes as Jav's fingers slid through his hair, his palm spreading wide on Stef's crown. "I do want you," Stef said. "At the same time, everything in me, in my head and my gut, it's all saying this is something good. Something unique and worth holding my horses for. Something worth being patient for. So I will."

"Holding your horses," Jav said. "Cool metaphor, Pony."

"Thanks."

"I don't want you to think I'm not attracted to you. Because I am. You turn me on and work me up. You get me so fucking hard sometimes. I go out of my mind wanting you and just when I think I'm ready to do something about it, I..."

"Panic?"

"No, I just *stop*. But it's not stopping out of fear. It doesn't feel fearful. It feels..."

Stef waited.

"It feels almost smug," Jav said, sighing. Then he chuckled. "I don't even know what that means."

"Smug," Stef said. He rolled toward the headboard, the side of his face burrowing into Jav's flank. Jav pushed fingers through Stef's hair, scratching a little. "Smug means pleased. Proud. Self-satisfied."

"And?"

"I don't want to put words in your mouth," Stef said. "I'm just thinking out loud here so push me off the bed if I'm full of shit. But maybe you stop because you *can* stop. Because money isn't part of whatever's happening with us here."

"Mm." The single exhaled syllable invited more.

"Let me ask you something," Stef said. "Did dates with your clients feel like constructing one complete love story, start to finish, within the span of a few hours? Like you went in as a stranger, but acting like you were already crazy about her? Already the perfect boyfriend and she was the perfect woman, no matter you'd never met before?"

"Kind of," Jav said slowly.

"So you packed the chase, the courtship, the amazing sex and the happily ever after into four hours, then took the envelope, turned the page and headed into the next story."

18

"With new clients, yes. Toward the end it was mostly regulars. So not so much starting new stories as continuing old ones. Serial love stories."

"That's a lot to juggle around in your head," Stef said. "That you're X in this story, but Y in that story. Being an escort kind of means being an actor."

"Not kind of," Jav said, smiling.

"You're like the ultimate understudy. Ready to step into any part at any moment, depending on what script your client gives you."

"Mm."

"And I'm not giving you a script," Stef said. "I'm not paying you. You don't have to stay. You don't have to do anything. You can just lie here and...be you. And part of you is smugly enjoying taking your sweet ass time figuring this all out. Makes sense to me."

"You make it sound so much cooler than what goes on in my head."

"My job is to make the mess in people's heads sound cool."

THE ROLE LONELINESS PLAYED

I'VE BEEN SLEEPING ALONE for so long.

Jav was never more aware of the role loneliness played in his life than when he slept with Stef. Literally slept. Sometimes with Stef curled against his back, sometimes with Stef's shoulder blades against his chest. Sometimes with nothing more than his little toe touching Stef's calf under the covers. But always that extra physical presence in constant contact through the night. After decades of sleeping solo, it ought to have been weird. A disruption of routine.

Jav loved it.

Christ, this is what it's like.

"I keep going back to that thing," Stef said, one night at Hickory's BBQ, as they demolished two-for-one ribs. "Of sex never being about you."

"What about it?"

"I mean, never like...*never*? Was that just in your work or in your personal life, too?"

Jav took his time chewing his last mouthful, along with the question he was reluctant to answer.

"How much of a personal sex life did you have anyway?" Stef asked, sucking sauce off his thumb. "I mean, if it's not too personal to ask."

"Not much. And to be honest... Any relationships I had with women felt like relationships with non-paying clients."

Stef's expression was thoughtful over his beer bottle. "Ever been tied up?"

"Pardon?"

"Ever been tied up in bed?"

"You mean literally?"

"Yeah."

Jav barked a laugh. "No."

Stef didn't laugh along. "You ever do the tying up?"

"Sure."

"Handcuffs?"

"Few times."

"Spanking?"

Defensiveness prickled at the back of Jav's eyeballs. "If she paid, I played."

"But you never had a client or a lover who wanted a night to call the shots or dominate you in any way?"

"No."

Stef's eyes softened into something that looked like sadness. "So it's fair to say that in the entire time you've been a sexually active male, which is...what, thirty years? Give or take?"

Jav nodded.

"You've never once *not* been in control in bed."

Looking at the table top, Jav shook his head. "No."

"Dude, think about that."

"I know." He looked up, and Stef was smiling now, the dimple creasing the side of his face.

"I don't mean this date to turn into therapy," he said. "You can punch me if I start to get too shrinky."

"Wait, this is a date?" Jav said.

Stef kicked him under the table. "Who took care of you all these years?"

"I took care of myself."

"But what if you... I don't know, broke your leg or something? What if you had a debilitating stomach bug. Did you have one person to bring you soup and sympathy?"

Jav shook his head. "You're making me think about things I never gave any thought to. If I got sick, I was sick. I powered through and took care of myself. If I broke my leg... I don't know, I guess I would've figured something out. Gloria would've helped me. My buddy Russ. I

21

mean, I had friends, but..."

"You had no one you let take control. No one who said 'poor baby.'"

Memory pressed on Jav's shoulders. "When I was living with Ari in Guelisten, we both got the flu. Val Lark actually did bring over soup for us. And Trelawney would send up this honey-lemon-ginger drink..."

Because we're your family, dumbass. We'd do anything.

Stef pulled another rib off the rack. "Crazy how much basic human connection was snatched away from you. At such a young age. It's not that much of a shock you fixed things so no one could ever do it again. But there I go being shrinky again."

Jav watched him eat, suddenly filled with memories of his mother fussing over him. Bandaging cuts and blowing on scrapes. A wrinkle of worry between her brows as she put a hand to his fevered head. Lighting the burner under the kettle to make a hot drink for a sore throat. He remembered her bringing him a soft-boiled egg and toast in bed, then pulling the covers high and telling him to rest. She ran a cold cloth on the back of his neck when he was throwing up his shoes, murmuring he'd feel better when it was over.

Rosa Gil deSoto was a prickly, difficult woman, but she took care of her own. Jav wasn't making the memories up. The recollections were true and they belonged to him. He was Rosa's only son and she loved him, tended to him and kept him safe.

Until it was all snatched away.

"I missed out on a lot," he heard himself say.

That night, he lay under Stef, fenced in by his tattooed arms and crushed by his tall, solid weight. When his wrists were held down to the mattress, he didn't fight. He tried to set aside words like *conquered* and *dominated* and *controlled*. To turn them inside out and connect with ideas like *shelter, protection, trust* and *safety*. To lie still and do nothing. Not being passive, rather being an active recipient. To just...

Enjoy it, he thought.

It took time for three decades of skin to slough off and new skin cells to emerge, but when they did, they were full of nerves and curiosity and electric interest. He held still and let Stef kiss him everywhere.

Everywhere.

Stef rolled him over and down and up and side-to-side, taking off his clothes and running his hands, mouth and face along every muscle, every angle and plane and curve and fold. Jav exhaled, letting go the long lonely years. Letting go his uncertainties and insecurities. Basking in the discovery what felt good to him and letting it feel good.

"Feels so good," he whispered, lolling under the strong hands that pushed his legs apart, coaxed his knees to bend up and out. Stef's kiss was soft in his mouth but his touch was immutable. It held Jav down, held him open, held him sprawled and splayed and vulnerable to the world.

"Feels so good."

He was hard all this time, but Stef hadn't touched him there yet. His hands moved along Jav's limbs, stroking and caressing and kneading. They dug into his hair and held his head still for kisses. The heat in Jav's blood built up and built up until he had to come or die. He closed fingers around Stef's wrist and moved their hands down between his legs.

"Touch me," he said. "Make me come. Feels so good."

Stef woke him up the next morning. Outside a torrential downpour of rain cracked like a hundred whips against the windows. Inside, Jav curled and cracked out of sleep. His head cradled in the crook of Stef's elbow while Stef's other hand slid down his chest and stomach. The pull of the drawstring and then Stef's fingers slid beneath the waist of his sweats, plunged in and took hold of him. His cock ached and twitched and howled in Stef's palm, wanting to come fast and hard.

Stef squeezed and stroked him, his thumb rolling in a circle at the tip and then sliding down the length again. He let go and slid his hand toward Jav's hip, moving his pants aside.

"Pull these down," he whispered against Jav's mouth.

Jav slid the pants down his legs, leaving them at his calves like loose bonds. Stef's hand pushed his knees open, ran in long strokes over his thighs, spreading him into a diamond and then taking hold of his cock again. He groaned into the kiss, biting and sucking.

"You want my hand or my mouth," Stef whispered.

"Your hand."

Stef reached for lube and his palm turned slippery and warm, like his kiss.

"So fucking hot," he said against Jav's lips.

Jav pushed his hips into Stef's grip, writhing and bucking. "You're making me come."

Stef's teeth closed on Jav's lower lip and pulled a little. "Show me." His hand slid faster, squeezed tighter.

"God," Jav cried. "Fuck..." It was on him and he torqued and twisted in Stef's relentless grasp, overflowing and pouring out hot as he was kissed into oblivion. The dark behind his eyelids unfolding and peeling away into gold.

"Feels so good," he said into Stef's mouth, over and over. "Feels so good, Finch. Feels so fucking good..."

SHRINKS & KINKS

THE COALITION FOR CREATIVE THERAPY didn't have enough players for their own softball team. They banded with the staff from a West Village head shop, and the resulting lineup called themselves the Shrinks & Kinks.

The official season went to mid-October. But this November weekend's forecast was irresistible: clear skies and high seventies. In a flurry of emails and texts, the team got Horatio Hardware's lineup to join them on Randall's Island for a last hurrah.

As the sun dipped down, the temperature dropped rapidly and the wind off Hell Gate turned fierce. Fleeces were pulled on and zipped high. Players blew on their ungloved fingers. At four o'clock, the field lights were already turning on.

Stef, playing second base, squinted to his left, where Jav was poised at first.

It was a no-brainer inviting him to play. Not even a question if he played. He was a Dominican-American growing up in Queens, of course he played fucking ball. With an unconscious, natural athleticism that was...

Hot.

Stef pounded a fist into his glove, refocusing for all of five seconds before his eyes drifted left again. Jav hunched, hands on knees, hips kicked out, watching the pitches. Unshaven, baggy sweats and cap backward. Two chicks sitting along the first base line were openly enjoying the view.

You like that? Stef thought with a smug exhale out his nose. *I sleep with it.*

He punched his glove harder. Hard enough to hurt and get his mind off the visual before he popped an infield boner.

Just in time, too. The batter hit a ground ball to second. Stef scooped it up and fired it across to Jav, who caught it easily and stepped on the bag. He lobbed it to Beau on the mound, his smile stretched wide, making Stef's chest tie itself up like a bow.

How the fuck did this happen?

In five weeks, Jav had slipped seamlessly into Stef's circle. Whatever the venue or activity, Jav was game. You mentioned tennis and sure, Jav played tennis. Golf? Absolutely. Squash, racquetball, handball—he was in. Jav could carry a half-dozen sports the way some people could carry a tune. What he lacked in practical skill he made up for in knowledge. He could talk skiing, sailing, surfing or hang-gliding with the same ease as baseball, hockey and basketball.

"It was part of the job," he said, shrugging. "Client wanted to scuba dive, so I got certified. If she wanted to ride horses on the beach, I rode. Go to a hockey game or go to the opera. Ballroom dancing or paint ball. If she paid, I played. Being an escort means being a yes man."

"Ever say no to anything?" Stef asked.

"Sky diving," Jav said, with a strangely sad smile.

Stef glanced at him sideways. "Before or after Nine Eleven?"

"Well, before I didn't really have a desire to jump out of a plane. But afterward... I didn't exactly have a phobia about flying after Nine Eleven, but I had really strong issues with falling through the sky."

Stef mused over Jav's impressive resume, thinking it couldn't be entirely built from necessity. Jav had a hungry mind. You had to work really hard to find a topic of conversation he couldn't engage in. If he wasn't informed about something, he was asking questions so he could *get* informed.

"In school, I was the kid who could deflect the teacher off topic," he said. "Reading *Tale of Two Cities*, I'd ask about guillotines. Teacher would forget Dickens and lecture on all of mankind's gushy methods of capital punishment for an hour. Girls were turning green and the guys couldn't get enough."

Besides being driven by imagination, Jav had an innate curiosity about the world, evident in his sharp powers of observation, his hundreds of questions and a genuine desire to learn. He was a fierce perfectionist when it came to his writing, but nearly everything else was for the amusing hell of it. Merely gaining passing knowledge of a new skill pleased him. Mastering it was beside the point. Even failure served a purpose.

"Bad decisions make good stories," he said.

He approached sexual exploration the same way. Once he voiced his hard limits, and his confused qualms about topping and bottoming were out of the way, he fell easily into bed, following where Stef slowly led. Getting comfortable with the fluidity, realizing Stef wasn't locking him into any one position or role.

"You're not the bitch in the arrangement," Stef said.

"Good to know," Jav said. "Take your clothes off."

Stef found getting Jav to trust him meant more than getting him naked. It wasn't so much how they moved in the throes as it was Jav lying *still* afterward. He stayed the night, or Stef stayed with him. Jav fell asleep asking questions, Stef nodded off mid-answer. They woke up, another day unfolded and the weight of Jav's trust settled a little more into Stef's hands.

He didn't know trust had this kind of mass. Jav's was a treasure unearthed. Weathered and golden, warm and heavy in Stef's palms. His fingers closed around it almost reverently, not sure when guiding Jav through this new sexual terrain had gone from an adventurous turn-on to a privilege. Stef's eyes rolled to the ceiling, denying any such bullshit, before they helplessly closed and admitting everything.

"You guys are getting serious," Stavroula said. A certain booth at the Bake & Bagel now had a *Reserved* sign on weekend mornings, waiting for its two regulars.

Serious, Stef thought, struggling to keep his head in the game as he wondered why *serious* was a word used to describe human relationships. Serious meant not fooling around, and a fuck-ton of that was going on. Serious meant things were grave or somber, but he and Jav cracked each other up.

"We take each other seriously," he said.

Stav smiled. "I've never seen you like this."

"It's never been like this."

He'd bump into Lilia in the front hallway and she'd ask, "Is your boyfriend coming to Sabbath dinner on Friday?"

"I saw someone reading your boyfriend's book on the subway," Rory said.

Your boyfriend.

I have a boyfriend, Stef thought, rolling the word round and round his mind. Jotting it on scraps of paper until the word looked foreign.

How did this happen?

I saw him across an empty gallery. I thought he was hot. I hoped we'd hook up and get naked. Have a good time and be on our way.

Now he's my boyfriend.

Jav seemed just as bewildered. Even with his trust safe in Stef's grasp, he still fell into pockets of his self-proclaimed idiocy. Mornings after hot nights when he'd sigh a lot, somewhere between pensive and brooding. At least the guy didn't bullshit Stef with "Nothing" when asked what was up.

"I'm all in my head," Jav said. "Being with you feels so good. It feels like me and it feels right and I love it. But sometimes my brain gets fixated on the..."

"On the *gay* part," Stef said.

"Yeah. It's cerebral. It's dumb. But, yeah, that's what it is."

The confused desire in anyone else would've irritated the shit out of Stef. Coming from Jav, he only wanted to protect it. "Don't forget this is the most time I've spent with a guy I sleep with," he said.

"So...are we friends with benefits?"

Stef crossed his arms. The doors of his heart had swung wide open, slamming back against his chest, and he needed that bit of barrier. "I've had fuck buddies," he said. "This is different."

"How?"

"Because when I visualize my week and map out my time, I'm starting to prioritize when I'll see you."

Jav's shoulders settled down. "Me too. You're a factor in my plans. I'm past the point of thinking you're a fun companion to do shit with. I'm starting to just want your time, and where we go or what we do is irrelevant."

"Which means, possibly, we're dating. Can you dig it?"

Jav smiled. "This is me digging it."

"Ball four," the umpire called, A smattering of applause as the batter from Horatio Hardware trotted out to first. Jav took off his cap, ran a hand through his hair and replaced it, bill forward this time.

"Stop fucking him with your eyes, Finch," Dominique said from shortstop.

"Can't," Stef said.

"Jesus, how do you leave the house?"

"Under great duress."

"Think people that beautiful know they're beautiful?"

Jav definitely knew. He'd be the first to admit he had a vain streak. And why not? The guy had gotten far with his looks and subconsciously or not, he still relied on his appearance to keep him where he was. He worked out religiously and dressed well. In fact, he was picky as fuck about his clothes. He liked looking good. He'd mastered the art of looking like he rolled out of bed half-gorgeous and threw the other half of himself together without giving a shit. But he gave quite a large one.

"It's a thing," he said. "I complain that people can't get past my looks, and at the same time I never give anyone the chance to get past them. I guess because for a long time, they were all I had." His sheepish expression became resigned. "Or hell, maybe I'm just a vain fuck."

Nice thing about dating a forty-five-year-old, their self-awareness was in place. And to be fair, looking at Jav didn't suck. For five weeks now, Stef had been cramming his eyes with the man. Jav at work and at play. Resting or running. Eating, sleeping, shaving, showering. Anxious, brooding, worked-up, let down, excited, frustrated. Coming and going. And best of all, looking right back at Stef.

"No puedo dejar de verte," he said from across the room, across the couch, the table, the bed.

I can't stop looking at you.

Their nights together were filled with wild heat, which filled Stef's work days with distraction, as torrid moments tapped his shoulder or intense memories sat in his lap. Besides curator and sailor, he was now a train of thought engineer, constantly concentrating on keeping the rig on the rails.

He wasn't alone in the daily derailments.

"I can't get shit done," Jav mumbled. "A thousand words a day has been my quota for years. A thousand is clearing my throat. Lately I can't get fifty on the page before I'm staring into space, thinking about you."

"Sorry," Stef said.

"Basically all I *do* is think about you. All damn day long."

"I take full responsibility."

"I'm so behind on this book it's ridiculous."

"Entirely my fault."

They were adults. They knew how to power through and do their jobs. It only took so many days of lost productivity before they laid down the law of no sexting during business hours. They tried the sensible step of spending at least two nights a week in their own beds, only to end up talking or texting all damn night and being useless the next day anyway.

The metallic crack of bat connecting with ball sliced through Stef's thoughts. It was a sound that could transport him instantly to middle school and manifest his father's voice from the bleachers.

Look alive, Finch.

The batter had aimed a grounder toward Dominique at shortstop, no doubt thinking the drag queen in yoga pants couldn't field. Wrong. Like liquid, the former Little League champ plucked the ball and flipped it to Stef at second. Stef touched the bag, pivoted on his heel and sent the ball screaming into Jav's glove. A flawless double-play to end the game. Horatio Hardware 7, Shrinks & Kinks 10.

"To the bar, ladies," Dominique called.

WHAT ABOUT MY ASSHOLE?

CHRIST, THOUGHT STEF, but the man could kiss like a motherfucker.

Had he, for want of a better word, *melted* like this when Courtney kissed him? When Quinn or Thomas or... *Oh hell, forget it.*

As his thoughts disintegrated, his hands climbed up the back of Jav's sweater, palms spreading wide to get as much of that skin as he could. His knees inched up Jav's hips, shifting and bucking to get their erections to rub just the right way. All the while kissing and kissing and kissing.

I haven't sucked face like this since I was a teenager.

Jav started laughing softly.

"What?" Stef said, sitting up. He followed Jav's gaze to Roman, who sat on his haunches. Head tipped to the side and expression curious.

One wonders what you are doing, master. May one participate as well?

"He's so confused," Jav said.

"I see the humans are mowing," Stef said, pushing his hair back in place. "I also enjoy mowing." He let out a groan as Jav's mouth found his neck. What he could do to a neck should've been illegal. An edge of teeth, a slide of tongue and a bit of suck Stef was sure would leave him with marks he'd have to explain at work. But Jav never left a trace.

At least not where anyone could see.

Stef dropped his hands on the small of Jav's back—warm and a little damp with excited sweat—then slid them down his jeans.

Who's the luckiest son of a bitch in the world?

His hands squeezed.

That would be me, ladies and gentlemen.

Whether in male or female company, Stef had never considered himself an ass man. His interest usually went to upper body first. His eyes checked out boobs, arms, abs and shoulders. Not necessarily in that order. Jav had serious torso game but this ass was in another stadium. Stef filled his hands and pulled Jav in more, grinding their hardness together. His fingers slid along the crack. Then slid in a little.

Jav yelped a laugh and bucked back, dragging Stef's wrists under the waistband.

"Ow," Stef cried. "Dude. Easy. Let go."

"Sorry," Jav said, still laughing as he came back down again. "That was just..."

"Too weird."

"No, it...tickled."

"Uh-huh." Stef crossed his smarting wrists over Jav's shoulders and bit on his ear. "Quite the knee-jerk reaction there, my friend."

Jav chuckled weakly. "Yeah, I... Yeah."

"Listen," Stef said.

"Oh, God. I killed the mood."

"Shut up."

"You're gonna be shrinky, aren't you?"

"I'm going to talk about your asshole for ten seconds, okay?"

Jav howled laughing then, rolling off Stef and tumbling to the floor. Roman came trotting over, ears perked up.

"Dude," Stef said, peering over the side of the couch. "I'm losing my erection."

"Sorry," Jav gasped, one hand over his face, the other rubbing Roman's head and neck. "Go ahead. What about my asshole? Talk slow."

"I'm not going to sneak a finger in when your guard's down, okay?"

"I know."

"My hands may go there but I'm not *going* there until you're ready. I'm not going to accidentally on purpose trip, fall down and whoops, sorry about the digits in your ass, Landes."

Jav exhaled out the last of the giggles. "I know. I mean my brain knows but I guess my body doesn't quite believe it yet."

"Well keep telling your bod that when it happens, it'll be because I asked if I could, or you asked if I would."

Jav looked up at him. "That's hot."

"Consent is hot." Stef drew a fingertip along Jav's mouth. "So is your asshole."

Jav reached up a hand, closed it around Stef's shirt and yanked him down to the floor. They rolled over the rug, laughing and pummeling. Roman circled them at a distance, watching, ears quivering and his head tilting this way and that.

One wonders if you are happy...?

CONFUSED DESIRE

"ALL THOSE YEARS," JAV SAID. "I said all kinds of things to all kinds of women. Sweet things. Sexy things. Dirty things. Everything. Anything. Or nothing. It wasn't scripted but I was just saying what the mood required. Reading a woman's vibe and saying what she needed to hear. It was never about me. Half the time I had some kind of story or narrative in my head to help me stay into it. But now with you...being me... It's not that I don't want to tell you stuff, but I... I don't know, man. It's like I'm fucking seventeen. Everything I feel literally gets stuck in my throat and I just stand here like a dork."

Stef slid arms around Jav's waist. "I get it."

"I know you do. That's another thing. I mean, God, I could be hooked up with some loser who *didn't* get it and I'd be feeling like an even bigger dork."

"You're not a dork."

"Admit it, I'm a dork."

"You're a hot, cool, funny, intelligent, talented, sexy and *awesome* dork," Stef said.

And right now, you're my dork, thank you very much.

Jav's smiling mouth opened, then closed around unspoken words.

Stef ruffled his hair. "Want me to leave you alone?"

"No. I've had enough of being alone. I just want you to bear with me."

"Newsflash, Landes: bearing with you is like my new favorite hobby."

"Smartass..."

They shoved and pummeled each other for a while. That

roughhousing with Jav brought him so much pleasure was something that got stuck in Stef's throat. He had a pretty good idea why his insides yapped like a hyperactive dog when Jav grabbed or tackled him. It woke up memories of childhood days when his father would wrestle with him. Or the few precious years when his older brother Nilas had a personality, and he'd chase Stef all through the house, finally tackling and tickling him. Stef had lived for those wild, laughing, brawling sessions. He made an eye-rolling show when he was hugged or canoodled, but he loved it. Loved the feel of his father's hands and his brother's weight. Too soon those carefree, physically demonstrative days came to an end. First he was told he was too old for it. Then too tall. And finally, the truth...

"Too gay," his middle brother Kurt said. "It's outright weird how you're all touchy-feely with guys. Knock that shit off. It's fucking embarrassing."

Maybe that's why I like sex with men, he thought, as he and Jav came to rest against the kitchen wall, the horseplay downshifting into kissing.

Maybe I'm just trying to recreate my childhood.

Or maybe I just fucking like it and Kurt can go suck a bag of dicks.

"What?" Jav said.

"What?"

"What are you giggling about?"

"Nothing," Stef said. "Everything."

"I know. I haven't laughed this much in a long time."

"It's my second-favorite hobby." Stef slid a hand beneath the hem of Jav's shirt, up the tight stomach and broad chest and out his collar. Jav slid down the wall a little. Still chuckling, but looking up at Stef with eyes full of confused desire.

"I have the fucking best time with you," Stef said, planting his palms flat to the wall and pinning Jav to it. Their panting laughter melted away as they kissed. Jav's hands moved up into Stef's hair and held on, turning his head around the kiss, moving him this way and that. Finding the best fit. Little noises in chests and throats.

"It's too good," Jav whispered. "You..."

"Tell me."

"You get me so fucking hard."

"I love that," Stef said, licking Jav's bottom lip.

"I swear, nothing's ever gotten me this worked up. And that makes me feel seventeen in the best way."

It was like sunshine on Stef's skin. "Unbuckle your belt."

A jingle and a small slap of leather as Jav obeyed. He went for his button but Stef took his hands and pinned them up high, kissing again, rubbing his erection against the bulge in Jav's jeans.

"Feel what you do to me?" he said, taking the lobe of Jav's ear between his teeth.

A breathy laugh. "Yeah."

Stef let go a hand and curled it around the back of Jav's neck. "Now open them."

He pushed Jav's shirt up while Jav's fingers unbuttoned and unzipped.

"Pull them down," Stef said. "Just your jeans."

His groin ached and throbbed as Jav pushed the denim down his legs and left them at his knees. Strong thighs and dark blue boxer-briefs, the outline of his hard cock tenting up and out to the right. Stef ran his hand along it, squeezed through the fabric, slid along that stiff length, forcing a grunt out of Jav's chest.

"You're hot with your clothes half off," Stef said.

"You fucking make me nuts."

Stef hooked his arm around Jav's neck, pulled his head in tight and kissed him. Mouth and tongue and teeth while his hand squeezed and slid and jerked Jav through his shorts.

"Mm-nn," he murmured when Jav reached for Stef's fly. "Not me yet. Just you."

Jav's hands dropped and his chest heaved for breath. His hairline was growing damp. His mouth sucked and bit hard as Stef tugged and teased at him. Sliding a hand down the back of his briefs and stroking it up the crack of his ass. Easing the waistband down a bit on one side. Then the other. Stef bent his head and ran his tongue around Jav's nipple, which rose up into a tight bead. He sucked hard and pulled Jav's pants down all the way. His cock sprung free and stood up high. Stef moved his hand up Jav's thigh, caught his balls in a palm and then gathered as much as he could hold in a fist.

"Feel good?"

Jav made some kind of assenting noise.

Stef buried his face in Jav's shoulder. "I think about this all day long at work. Coming home and doing things to you."

"So do I."

"I spend half my time with a hard-on for you."

"Same. I…"

"What?'

Jav swallowed, hesitation making his muscles seize under Stef's body.

"It's okay," Stef said softly, running his teeth gently along Jav's skin. "I won't laugh."

"Want your mouth."

Stef slid Jav's shirt up and over his head, then took Jav's jaw in his palms and kissed him hard. "Say more."

Through the feverish kissing, Jav said more. "I want your mouth on my cock."

Stef crouched on his heels, letting his hands trail down Jav's body and pulling the rest of his clothes off. "I'll just warn you up front," he said, putting his face into Jav's skin and inhaling.

"What?"

"I suck at this."

Jav barked a laugh, which melted into a groaning sigh as Stef wrapped his mouth around him. Stef rocked down on his kneecaps, eyes closed and his concentration pulled deep within. He didn't just want this to feel good. He wanted it to be the best fucking head Jav got in his *life*.

"Christ," Jav whispered, threading fingers through Stef's hair.

Stef sank his consciousness into Jav, going down on himself as well, doing what felt good to him. Listening to what made Jav hiss his breath in, what made the fingers in Stef's hair clench, and what made him go limp and sink into the wall.

"Jesus Christ."

Stef paused for breath. "Feel good?"

"Feels like the worst blow job ever."

"Sorry." He took Jav in again, exhaling slow and relaxing so he could get him all the way into his throat. Holding Jav there a long wet moment.

Then releasing him out, spit-slick and hard like gold. His hand cupped around Jav's balls and squeezed, the other hand wrapping around the shaft, feeling the veins pulse beneath the smooth skin. "God, I want to make you come," he said, the tip pressed against his chin.

"I'm so fucking close."

"Are you?"

A wet click as Jav swallowed hard and nodded. "Can I come in your mouth?"

"Oh *hell* yeah." But he ran his mouth up Jav's stomach and chest, standing up to glide his tongue along Jav's throat and catch his mouth in a kiss he put his soul into.

"I love hearing you ask for what you want," he said. "You know why?"

"Why?"

"Because you've never done it before."

One side of Jav's upper lip twitched. Then a corner curled into a lopsided, wicked grin under Stef's mouth. "I want you to suck me off," he whispered.

Stef's groin tightened like a clenched fist and he rubbed up hard against Jav's hip. "What else?"

Jav's teeth closed on Stef's lower lip, then let go. "I want to stop talking."

Stef carefully pulled away and dropped back onto his knees, happier than he'd been in years.

LATER THAT NIGHT, Stef lay on the couch in the dark living room. Sprawled naked in the cushions with Jav between his knees, and Jav was going down on him.

He's fucking going down on me.

He's never done this before in his life.

It was almost too much to think about. Definitely too much to look at. If he watched, he'd come in six seconds. He kept his eyes closed, feeling out the moment with all his other senses. The smell of his own desire, thick and earthy, like a forest floor. His tongue pressed to the roof of his mouth, tasting what he knew Jav could taste. Hearing the soft hum in Jav's chest and little sucking noises. The cool, soft dryness of Jav's hair through his fingers. And the softer, hot wet of his mouth.

God, his mouth.

Stef opened his eyes. A bit of streetlight sliced through the curtains and threw a beam across the couch, lighting up the curve of Jav's back. The sliding planes of his shoulders. The shape of his mouth and the hollow of his cheek. The dark crescent of his closed eyes. Behind them, what was he thinking? Feeling? Deciding?

He's never done this before.

Jav's open mouth slid along the length, up and over the tip. His tongue circled. He held still, drawing a breath through his nose. Then slowly his head sank down.

"Fuck," Stef whispered through the wall of his teeth. Orgasm stirred to life at the base of his spine, a Pegasus spreading wings out through his groin, squeezing and sucking from inside. Jav nudged under one of Stef's knees, scooping a calf up onto his shoulder. He moved in closer. Tighter. Hotter. Wetter. A strong hand wrapped around the base of Stef's cock. His other hand slid up Stef's side and twined with his fingers. Knuckles tight. Tendons straining in the skin.

"It's getting there," Stef said. "I'll tell you when."

Jav gave a grunt and nodded into Stef's lap but didn't say anything. He seemed to be doing fine.

Jesus, he was doing *great.*

Any other guy and Stef would've made a teasing joke over his head. *You sure you've never done this before?*

A rush of cool air followed by Jav's slow wet pant against Stef's stomach.

"All right?" Stef whispered.

"Mm. I keep forgetting to breathe."

No, he's never done this before.

Jav went after him again and Stef closed his eyes, feeling it start to bring him around.

God don't have been lying to me I don't want to know don't tell me just tell me I'm the first one...

His mind was coming apart while his body drew in close and small and tight.

Say I'm the only one and let me keep this mine keep it for me keep it in your mouth me for me please your mouth just for me—

"Now," Stef said hoarsely, the hand in Jav's hair tightening hard and pulling him off. Pulling him up. Pulling his mouth in, sucking on his tongue as Stef's other hand wrapped around Jav's slippery fingers. Together they stroked Stef the rest of the way, up and out and over. Holding on tight, shivering and shuddering down. Twitching into stillness.

"Jesus," Stef said.

"Dude, let go my hair," Jav whispered.

Stef's fingers sprang open. "Oh God, shit, I'm sorry."

"It's okay." Jav collapsed on Stef's chest, both of them heaving hard heavy breaths. Jav's back was damp with sweat, the tattoo between his shoulder blades fluttering.

"Holy fuck," Stef said.

"I know."

"Jesus, man, you suck worse than I do."

"I didn't want to show you up the first time."

"Thanks."

"Well..." Jav blew his breath out and rubbed his forehead against the ball of Stef's shoulder. "I enjoyed that more than I thought I would."

Stef rested his cheek against him, shaking his head at the universe's smug expression. "Me too."

This cannot be real. This cannot be happening.

He tightened his arms around it. Tucked his chin over Jav's shoulder, pinning him close. Hooked a heel into the back of Jav's leg, locking him in.

"I could fall asleep right here," Jav said. "Everything about you is just so damn easy."

All at once, the room swam warm and wet. Stef opened his mouth to answer but the words got stuck in the back of his throat.

Shh, the universe said. *Let him talk.*

A LITTLE SPRING

THE NIGHT TREMBLED, pink and anxious. Stef exhaled as Jav carefully slid a fingertip inside him.

"Oh my fucking God..."

"All right?"

Three little chuckles from somewhere deep inside Stef's chest.

"I'll take that as a yes." Jav's heart thudded in his ears as Stef pulsed around his finger. Smooth and hot and *tight*, Jesus Christ, like a tiny suction clamping his knuckle still.

"Come in more," Stef said. "It's good."

Jav moved his finger, up to the second knuckle now in that heated vacuum of hot space.

"Bit more," Stef said. "Curl up a little with your fingertip. *Yeah...*" His entire voice fell apart, replaced by a gasping laugh.

"That?" Jav said, moving his finger around a soft little bump. It had an easy spring to it, like the tip of a nose.

Stef made a garbled sound. He clenched down and his foot on the bed curled tight.

Thrumming with a slick power, Jav leaned and ran his tongue along Stef's cock. Up to the tip and down again. Filling his lungs with the scent of skin and sex. A purring moan in his own chest as he gathered the head into his mouth.

Welp, it's official, he thought. *I crave dick.*

He closed his eyes as the shape of Stef filled his lips and glided behind his teeth, making his own cock stand up in sympathetic interest.

And it's official. I don't give a shit what anyone thinks.

The power surged and he sucked harder, timing it with the slide of his finger. Tuning into Stef's groans, the twist of his shoulders and the rise of his hips to meet Jav's mouth.

"It's gonna make me come really fast," he said thickly. "And really hard."

Jav hummed, his eyes closed, his entire being on fire. "Good."

"I'll try to warn you."

"Don't worry about me." Bold and brave, he pushed up on his free hand and leaned long to kiss Stef's mouth. "I've been wondering what you taste like anyway."

"Oh Jesus, man."

Jav slid a second finger into him. "Okay?"

"Little more lube."

Jav applied it and got his fingertips up against that little knob of nerves. "There?"

Stef's knees fell open and his hand reached to touch Jav's head. "Stop talking."

Jav pulled him into his mouth and pushed his fingers in. His own cock was up high in his lap, dripping with jealous curiosity, wanting in on the action. As he slid in and out of Stef, and Stef slid in and out of him, his own butt was clenching and flexing and imagining.

This is interesting. I think I want to check this out.

When Stef came, it was with his entire body. Every cell, every hair standing up straight and pounding its chest. His voice turned inside-out until it was nothing but a hoarse, stuttered moan above the bed. As a salty-sweet rush flooded Jav's mouth, he could feel the veins pulse, both against his tongue and around his finger. Stef went on coming, twitching and trembling and gasping wetly through his teeth. Laughed curses and his hands raked tight in his hair.

He came, it seemed to Jav, forever.

"Jesus *Christ*, it feels so fucking good," he said, his legs finally going limp.

Oh yeah, Jav thought, transfixed and staring. *I definitely want to check this out.*

Come Here, You Moron

"Come to bed?" Jav said.

"I gotta finish this report. Half an hour, okay?"

Jav nodded. "And maybe..." He rolled one hand in the air in an ambiguous gesture.

"Is that a take a walk on the wild side...?" Stef mimicked the gesture.

"Maybe."

"Cool." Stef messed up Jav's hair and sat down at the desk.

Jav went into the kitchen and then came out, crossed his arms and dug a shoulder into the doorframe. "I'm gonna ask you something dumb."

"Hit me."

"Don't laugh. In fact, don't even look at me. Look at your computer. Work and listen."

Stef turned away in his chair. "I'm looking and I'm working. The laughing part of my brain isn't listening to you."

"Is there anything I need to do?"

"Do?"

"I mean to get ready."

Stef started to look back "I'll–"

"Don't look at me."

"I'll get you ready," Stef said to his bulletin board.

"That's not what I mean."

Three beats of confused silence before clarity smacked Stef between the eyebrows.

"Oh," he said. "No. No, there's nothing you need to do. Not for me.

No."

"All right. I just..."

Stef picked up a pencil and bent over a pad of paper, pretending to write. "If you're self-conscious and it makes you feel better, help yourself to the stuff under the sink. Or even a soapy finger up your butt once or twice is fine."

"Okay."

"Can I look at you please?"

"No."

Stef pushed back and spun in his chair. "Fucker, I can't not look at you." He stood up. "Come here, you moron. " He walked over to Jav and wound arms around his waist. "Look at me."

"No," Jav said, the color high along his cheekbones and his smile curling up shy and dorky. Such raw and vulnerable uncertainty in this gorgeous guy who used to get *paid* to fuck, made Stef want to die. The sheer, incredulous *luck* of it all made the marrow of his bones feel like it would explode.

"You are ridiculous," Stef said, hugging him.

"I'm *new* at this," Jav said.

"And I'm new at being with someone who's new at this so we're both new at this. And I don't care if it takes a year for you to get okay with...this. I don't care what we do or don't do in bed. Just don't ask me not to look at you. I'm not okay with that."

Jav glanced at him, then flicked his eyes away. "All right, you can look at me."

Stef kissed his face. "Gee, thanks."

"I'm gonna jump in the shower and think about things."

"I will be working. Here. And not thinking about anything."

Stef sat down carefully, adjusting the half-chubber in his jeans. Behind him he heard the bathroom door close. Then open.

"Wait," Jav said. "Is it one soapy finger up twice, or two soapy fingers up once?"

"Javier."

"Sorry." The door closed.

Stef closed his eyes and thought about everything.

A little while later, Jav came out, fresh and wet-haired, old sweats and a T-shirt. He leaned and put his chin on Stef's shoulder.

"May I help you?" Stef said.

"Go back to the I'll get you ready thing?"

Stef half turned his head and whispered, "When you're ready, I'll get you ready."

"That's hot."

"You wait..."

The kiss was interrupted by Stef's cell phone ringing. Ronnie Danvers' number on the display. Calling at nine o'clock at night, which was never a good thing.

Oh, Christ, it's Geno, he thought.

INTO THE SOFTNESS

Chaow, the Thai teenager at Exodus Project, had a bigger role in earlier drafts. In fact he was in the basement with Geno and Carlos. But he pulled the story in too many directions so ultimately his part was reduced. He brought me soup and forgave. —SLQR

"HE WANTS YOU," Ronnie said on the phone. "Can you come?"

Stef squeezed his eyes tight, his sexy plans with Jav falling in pieces on the floor. Chaow was dead. Geno went down to the kitchen for a snack and found Chaow dead, his wrists slit. Now he was upset, triggered and distraught. And he wanted Stef.

"I have to go," Stef said.

"Of course," Jav said, pale above his tightly-crossed arms. "He needs you."

"I'm sorry," Stef said, shrugging on his jacket.

"Don't be. This is more important."

Stef managed a curt nod. "I'll be back as soon as I can."

"Don't worry. I'll be here."

From the door, Stef looked back over his shoulder. "Promise?"

Jav slid arms around him from behind and squeezed him tight through one shared inhale and exhale. "I won't go anywhere. I'll walk the dog, that's it. Call me if you need anything."

It was after midnight when Stef got home. Jav was reading on the couch.

"You didn't have to wait up," Stef said, setting his keys down on the counter.

"I promised." He walked over to Stef but didn't touch him. The dishwasher swished and splashed as they looked at each other.

"You all right?" Jav finally asked.

"Remember I said I'd tell you when it was one of those nights I needed to be fucked back to myself?"

Jav nodded.

"It's not one of those nights."

"Do you want me to go?"

"Yeah, I need you to go," Stef said. "I need to be by myself."

Still nodding, Jav took a small step back. Stef followed and put a hand on his arm.

"Remember I also said I'd act like I don't want you around but I do?"

"Mm."

"That's what's happening right now."

"I know." Jav took Stef's gloves off and unzipped his jacket. Slung it aside and folded Stef into his arms. "I won't talk, I won't ask you questions. I'll get in your face or I'll stay out of your way. I'll hold you all night or I'll sleep on the couch. I'll do whatever you want. But I won't leave."

"I just need to get it off me," Stef said against his shoulder.

Jav stripped him down right there in the living room, then took him into the shower. Stef stayed behind closed eyes, turning into the spray and lifting limbs one at a time to be scrubbed.

"Just let me be a few minutes," he said when they were in bed.

"Do whatever you have to do."

Stef rolled away from him, curled on his side around a couple of pillows. Breathing through his mouth into the softness. Letting a mist of tears squeeze out until the fabric was damp with his failure and sadness and anger.

Behind him, he could feel Jav's deep, even breathing. Like the slow bellows of a forge. Warm and close. Watchful, but at a distance.

After a long, tired time, Stef rolled over and slid close to his lover. He kept his arms crossed tight over his chest, just resting his forehead against the side of Jav's arm.

"Warm enough?" Jav said softly.

"Mm. Thanks for staying."

"I wouldn't leave. Not tonight."

"You know you're my best friend."

A hand stroked his hair. "I do now."

Stef pressed his mouth against Jav's shoulder and sighed. "Sorry we didn't get to mess around."

Jav gave him a little shove, his smile flashing in the dark. "It's not important."

"It is. You're as important to me as my job."

They lay still a few minutes.

"So I was thinking," Jav said.

"Mm?"

"I'm going to go get blood drawn tomorrow. You know. Get tested."

"All right. I will too. I'm overdue for a physical anyway."

"It's time. I mean, since we seem to be heading down that road."

"Are you worried?"

"About the road or my test results?"

"Both."

"No. Are you?"

"No. But since we're having this conversation... Even if results are negative, I'll still want to use condoms. No matter who's topping. I don't know, it just puts my mind at ease."

"I get it. I imagine the less on your mind, the more enjoyable it is."

"Exactly."

"Cool."

A long beat of silence. "I love you," Jav said, just as Stef said, "I love you."

Stef took his extra pillow and smashed it on Jav's face.

"Get out of my head, Finch," Jav said, knocking it away and laughing.

"Glad we had this little chat."

Jav gently ran his palm from Stef's forehead down the bridge of his nose, smoothing his eyelids shut. "Ve a dormir, pinzon."

BLOOD

I was bummed to see this scene go from *Finches*. I wrote it with one hand tied behind my back and I loved how it fleshed out the family Jav constructed to replace the one he lost. But in the end, in the interest of pacing and word count, it was cut.

Hey, what's that moan of regret about? —SLQR

JAV HAD BEEN GOING to the same Open Door clinic on 165th Street for over twenty years. Full STD screening every three months. Yearly physical. Flu shot. A typhoid vaccination when a client hired him for a trip to Costa Rica.

He appreciated both the sliding pay scale and the anonymity when he was in his twenties. The nurses were impartial and businesslike. Nothing shocked them. Maybe their eyes softened as they took note of his age, but they didn't judge as they drew blood and delivered his results which were, knock wood, always clean. In fact, knock more wood, other than common colds, occasional bugs and chronic neck strain from writing, Jav had rudely good health and he took care to keep it that way.

As he matured, so did his relationship with the practitioners, some of whom grew older right along with him. As years went by and pictures were pinned and repinned on the clinic's bulletin board, Jav asked after spouses and babies, sympathized when staff broke up with a lover or lost a parent. By the time he reached his thirties, he could've found a doctor in a more upscale medical practice, but he kept going to Open Door. They were his family.

Soleil Dalcide had been at the clinic at least twelve years. Gossip was her hobby and when her Haitian accent wasn't filling Jav's ears with juicy intrigue, it was nagging him to the point where it was almost flirtatious. But when he came in today, she burst into tears.

"Oh Jav, thank *God*," she said, putting a hand on his arm.

"What's the matter?"

"What's the matter?" she cried. "You're in here every twelve weeks like clockwork. You were due in August and you didn't show up, I thought…"

Jav blanched. "No, no, no, I'm fine."

"I thought you were *dead*."

"Oh my God, don't cry. I'm sorry."

She slapped his arm, then caressed it again. "I was so worried."

"I'm sorry. No, I'm fine. Don't cry."

"I know I shouldn't get attached. But I've known you so long now."

"I'm sorry. I'm fine. I'm here." Handing her a tissue, he felt like shit. Touched as hell. But still shitty. "I retired," he said. "I'm not working anymore."

"You're not?" she said, wiping her eyes.

"I'm out of the business. I'm here because I met someone."

"Oh, Javi," she said, blowing her nose. "How wonderful. Who is she?"

Jav worked at a scuff on the floor with the toe of his sneaker before looking back up at her. "He."

"He?" Her eyebrows went up a moment, then drew down in a hard, business-like stare. "Oh, Javier," she said. "We have to talk then."

"We do?" he said, as he was dragged into an exam room. Not by the ear, but it sure as hell felt like it.

"You need to be careful," Soleil said, an index finger raised.

"When have I never been careful?"

"You must use condoms."

Jav turned his fingertips to touch his chest. "Sol, this is me. Jav.

Former hustler. We've met, remember?"

The finger wagged menacingly. "Condoms every single time, Javier. Do you top or bottom?"

He crossed his arms. "Well, that's a little personal."

"You can contract HIV giving or receiving."

"I know."

"And lubricant. I cannot stress enough. You can easily damage the anal tissue which makes it more susceptible to sexually transmitted diseases."

"You're actually embarrassing me," Jav said.

"Make sure it is water-based. Oil-based can damage the condoms." She turned to the cabinets, flung them open and began rifling within. "KY is best. I'll give you some before you leave."

Jav's face swelled with stifled laughter as he pushed his tongue into his cheek. "Thank you."

"Roll up your sleeve."

"Yes, ma'am."

"Do you know the signs of herpes?" She stretched her fingers into a new latex glove in a way that turned Jav's pucker factor to eleven.

"I'll Google them."

Too late, she was already gathering pamphlets from the rack by the door and piling them next to his leg. "How many partners has your boyfriend had?"

"I haven't asked for a headcount."

"Has he been tested?"

"No. I mean, yes," he added when she glared at him. "Yes, in his lifetime but no, not since he and I have been dating. Which hasn't been long. And technically we haven't done...it."

"Have you had mouth-to-genital contact?"

I am forty-five years old, he thought, squirming like an eighth grader in health class while memories of said contact made his face flame. "Well..."

"You've done it. Make a fist." Soleil tied the piece of rubber tubing around Jav's bicep and started tapping the crook of his elbow, looking for a vein. "And speaking of fists, you—"

"Whoa," Jav barked. "Do *not* go there."

Now her mouth twisted around a giggle. "You must be careful," she said, more kindly now.

"I will be."

"You're really not working anymore?"

"No."

Now she sighed. Jav eyed her sideways.

"What's that moan of regret about?" he asked.

She swabbed him with the alcohol. "I was going to hire you for a date when I turned fifty."

"Fifty?" Jav said. "I'll be eighty-two."

She blushed, then jabbed him with the needle. "Oh, I should discuss prostatitis symptoms with you as well."

"Please don't."

WATER PLAY

"I'M TELLING YOU," Jav said, "I feel violated."

Stef was reading over the herpes brochure. "Soleil obviously loves you."

"She bruised me." Jav regarded the crook of his elbow, looking like he'd just bitten into a lemon.

"Poor baby."

"I walked out of there knowing way more about anal elasticity than I needed to."

"As if you weren't already a font of useless information."

Opening a beer, Jav went on complaining in an exaggerated Haitian accent. "Have you done it, Javier? Do you top or bottom? Have you had mouth-to-genital contact, Javier? Don't share your sex toys, Javier."

He slammed the fridge door, muttering in Spanish now. Stef caught "maldita madre," one of Jav's frequent expressions. A lot of his curses involved mothers. Stef wasn't sure if that was a Queens thing, a Latino thing or a Jav-has-unresolved-mommy-issues thing.

Stef put aside the brochures and poked into the white paper bag and its generous assortment of lube samples. "This is a rather charming side of you, Landes."

"Thank you. I save it for the special people in my life."

Stef rubbed a bit of the new Astroglide X between his thumb and index finger. His eyebrows went up as he checked the tube's fine print: *Great for water play!*

"Nice," he said.

"What?"

"Nice," Stef said louder. "I made the grade." He put all the goodies back in the bag and rolled the top down. Settling back on the couch, hands behind his head and feet on the coffee table, he regarded Jav who was now standing by the French doors. Outside it was pouring rain, grey and miserable. Jav's rust-colored thermal shirt was a splash of paint against the gloom. It fit tight in some places, leaving no doubt, and draped in other places, making Stef imagine things.

Like water play.

And leaving a testimonial on Astroglide's website: *Works great in the rain, highly recommend.*

"What's so funny?" Jav said.

"Nothing. Are you done being an idiot?"

Jav took a swig of his beer and glared. "No."

"When you're through being offended..." He shook the paper bag with his best Bambi eyes. "We have unfinished business from the other night, remember?"

Jav shrugged but when he went for another chug of beer he was smiling.

"Javito," Stef said, getting up.

"Don't call me Javito. You sound so white."

"Come here, you moron." Stef slid arms around Jav's waist and dug his chin into Jav's shoulder.

"Why do I like when you call me a moron?"

"Because the moron in me recognizes the moron in you."

"Namoronste?"

"Exactly. Now cheer up or I'll kill you."

"I'm perfectly cheery."

"How about I start celebrating without you," Stef said, sliding a hand down the front of Jav's jeans. "You can catch up when you're ready. Oh, look." His fingers squeezed what was growing hard within. "Nice of you to join us."

"Smartass."

Stef ran his mouth up Jav's neck and stopped at his ear. "You love it."

Jav's eyes closed, beer bottle poised at his open lips. "So does your mother."

"Y tu mama tambien."

"God, your accent sucks."

"So do you, when you're not being an idiot."

"Why don't you put your mouth where I used to make my money?"

"Oh I'll put more than that." Tugging Jav by the hem of his shirt, Stef picked up the paper bag. "Hit the shower, Landes, it's time for clinical trials."

"What am I, a lab rat?"

"You know it."

And in a scuffle that was half passionate clinch, half wrestling, they were dragging each other down the hall, bumping off the walls and shedding clothing. Laughter giving way to more blunt, impatient noises, until Stef went silent and Jav was cursing at the bathroom ceiling.

"Jesus fucking Christ," he cried, hands in his wet hair. "The fuck is that?"

"That would be your prostate, my friend."

"I *know*, but goddamn..."

"I can't believe you never had a woman do this to you."

"Only my primary care provider. And it felt nothing like this."

"Like...this?" Stef curled his finger again, knowing he had it when Jav's feet clenched, looking for purchase on the bottom of the tub.

The toes never lied.

"Holy shit, that's crazy."

"Want me to stop?"

"I'll fucking kill you if you stop."

Stef laughed. "Then you better hold onto something. You're about to lose some brain cells."

His blood crackled. He was high on power and prowess. Drunk on the thrill of being The First. The Only. The One. Making Jav writhe against the tiles, choking on his own cries, reaching here and there to grab onto anything and not even having the strength to curl his fingers.

"Feels so good," he said, gasping. His hand dropped on Stef's head. Then the other hand. Stef went still within the desperate grip. He let Jav take his head and come like a tornado. Come in a twisting frenzy, yelling through the shower spray, loud enough to wake up Hell's Kitchen.

They went still a long moment, Stef still on his knees, his face against

Jav's stomach.

"Dude, let go my hair."

"Oh shit." Jav's fists sprung open. "I'm sorry."

"Quite all right."

They dried off and fell onto the bed. Stef ran a hand in circles on Jav's chest. Feeling the hammer of his heart beneath. "How'd that feel?"

"Like the worst blow job ever," Jav said. He lifted up Stef's arm and rolled beneath it, curling on his side. "God, that sucked."

"Sorry. I'll never do it again."

"I'll kill you."

Stef stroked Jav's back, still a little damp, the tattoo between his shoulder blades fluttering. Jav blew his breath out and rubbed his forehead against the ball of Stef's shoulder.

"I never came like that in my life."

Stef rested his mouth against Jav's wet hair. He looked out beyond the plain of his bed and slowly shook his head at the universe.

This cannot be real. This cannot be happening.

As usual, the universe shrugged back at him with a smile. *Yet here we are.*

Some Beautiful Day

A RAINY, LAZY AFTERNOON. The playlist had shuffled through twice. The bedroom was dark except for the little light on Stef's corner shrine.

"So happy," Jav mumbled.

"Are you?"

"Mm."

Stef's hand slowly slid up and down Jav's back. "You, know, you're like...oddly hairless."

Jav hummed again.

"Is this the Gil deSoto heritage? Or the way you've groomed yourself to look?"

"Little of both," Jav said. "My father and his oldest brother were two wildebeests. Hair poking out of their undershirts and all that. But their middle brother, Kiko, his nickname was heuvo."

"Egg?"

"Mm. He was hairless. He could go for days without shaving and still be smooth. My dad said his father was the same way. But his father's brother was born with a mustache. So there's some deSoto gene going on that makes some of us beasts and some of us eggs."

The hair on Jav's thighs was dark, but it was short and fine. Below his knees it grew a little longer and started to gather above his skin. A down of the same fine hairs was in his lower back while his butt was nearly as smooth as his shoulders.

"Wonder if it's a Native American throwback," Stef said.

"Could be." Jav rolled on his side, his fingers running a circle around his sternum and a small, random patch of those fine hairs. "I used to wax this off."

"Why?"

His fingernails scratched his chest. "Because I'm a vain fuck."

Stef's fingers joined in the caress. "Leave it now. Let it grow."

"Why, you like it?"

"Doesn't matter what I like. I just want you to be you. You know? You don't have to be so perfect anymore. You don't have to look good all the time. Not for me, anyway."

Jav's mouth did that funny thing it did when he wanted to say something but he stopped to measure and weigh the words.

"What?" Stef said softly, running his thumb along Jav's bottom lip.

Jav closed his eyes, which he did when he was being brave. "I like looking good for you."

"You always look good to me."

"Yeah, but... Christ, what do I mean?" Jav ran a hand over his head. "When I want to...look nice for you or whatever, when I want to do things to please you, I mean them this time. I don't want or expect anything in return. I like doing it for the liking."

Stef pushed up on an elbow and kissed him, eyes open, taking slow, soft bites of Jav's mouth. Eating every word, every exhale, every brave act.

"See, when you're up over me like this?" Jav said, running a hand through Stef's hair.

"Yeah?"

"You're like..." His mouth trembled.

"Tell me."

"You're like the most beautiful thing I've ever seen."

Stef fell back to his side. Now it was his mouth that became a scale. *Beautiful* on one pan, words piling up on the other, weighing honesty against vulnerability. How much was too much. How much wasn't enough.

"Just...this," Jav said, running a hand down Stef's arms, then up again and over his shoulder and chest. "Your body. This."

His palm glided down Stef's stomach, fingers spreading to fit between ribs before caressing a path over his hip.

"This is beautiful to me."

His hand squeezed a glute. Then a quad. The backs of his fingers ran along Stef's penis, sliding between his thighs, cupping a moment then running up his stomach.

"As a man, I mean," Jav said. "How you look and feel and how you're put together. It turns me on. I'm finally in a place where I can comfortably say a man's body turns me on. I'm attracted to this. And it's okay that I am. I'm letting myself be attracted to it and the more I let, the more it...becomes beautiful to me." A corner of his mouth lifted in a wry grin. "I just feel weird saying so. Sometimes. It's dumb, but I guess parts of my brain still think some words are girl words and I can't say a man is beautiful."

Stef's hands roamed and glided and squeezed. "I don't think I've ever wanted a man to see me as much as I want you to," he said. "You look at me and... I'm me. And that's fucking beautiful."

The pans of the scales balanced. He was hard now, twitching and dripping.

"Come on top of me," Jav whispered. "Come up here. Let me look at you."

Kissing, Stef slung a leg over and rolled, rising up on his knees over Jav's legs. He set his cock next to Jav's and gathered them both up tight in his hands.

"God I love that," Jav whispered.

"What?"

"When you rub us together. Feels so good."

"I know."

"Does this have a name?"

"Um. I've heard 'brosturbate' once or twice."

Jav laughed, deep and wicked in his chest.

"Frottage," Stef said. "I think that's said in nicer circles."

Jav reached for the lube bottle and dripped some on them. "What should we call it?"

"You're the wordsmith," Stef said. "You pick."

They both let out a little groan as Stef's grip turned slick.

"Shit, I don't have a word for any of this," Jav said.

Stef moved his tightly cupped hands up the length of both of them, squeezing at the tips.

"Jesus," Jav whispered.

Stef let them go and pitched forward on his palms, leaned to lick the hollow at Jav's throat, then drop a secret into it. "God, I want to fuck you so bad."

"I know." Jav's hands threaded through Stef's hair. "Somed—"

"I know someday. Actually I don't care someday or not. But I want what I want. And it's easy to say so."

"I want to know you want it. I need to know that. I like knowing that. The more I'm with you and the more I hear it, the more curious I get."

"Yeah?"

"Yeah. Every time it's like... I get more used to the idea. Like I'm starting to see it. It's an easier and easier thing to picture and it gets more and more...appealing."

"That's why I want to wait," Stef said, hips moving like a dolphin as he rubbed them together. "I want to wait until that picture is so big and bright, so vivid in your head that..."

"What?"

Stef dropped down on his elbows, Jav's face in his hands. "That you *ask* me for it."

Jav kissed him. "I know I'm going to. Someday."

"Some beautiful day."

Kind of Loving You

JAV GOT TO CUSHMAN ROW and found a note on the kitchen counter: *Bad day. On the roof. Come find me. On second thought, you might want to run like hell...*

Jav went up the four flights of steps, one last wooden stairway and out into the cold night. Remembering a blistering hot night when he was seventeen. He and his cousin Ernesto scampering up to the roof with a stolen bottle of Dominican magic, neither knowing what it would cost them.

I went up to the roof a boy and got thrown down the stairs a man.

Stef sat on top of the air conditioning vent, forearms wrapped around his knees, staring out toward the West Side Highway and the Hudson.

"Hey," Jav said.

"Hey."

"You all right?" Jav said.

"I will be. Today was just tougher than usual."

"I'm sorry."

"When it's bad like this... None of my usual methods work. I just have to let it leave me when it's ready to."

"I get it."

"If I fight it, it sticks around longer. It just has to pass through like a storm."

"It's all right."

"It can get ugly. And I've never had anyone watch while it was happening."

"Do you want me to go?"

"No, I don't want you to go, but I don't exactly know how to have you here."

Jav climbed up on the vent and sat behind Stef. Drawing Stef between his knees to lean on his chest. Two bobsledders over Manhattan. Stef was rigid and tight in Jav's arms. Fits of trembling washed over him then left. A quake of them. Then stillness. And another shivering shake. His breath made choppy clouds in the air.

"Jesus, this kid is six years old..."

"Shh." Jav set his temple against Stef's. "You can't tell me."

"I know, but God, man, he's so little. And that long road of years in front of him..."

Jav pressed his head to Stef's. "Shh." He spread his palms wide around Stef's forearms, trying to make everything about himself firm and unyielding and immutable.

"You do what you can to keep it from sinking into your pores," Stef said. "But it's inevitable."

"You breathe it in."

"Yeah."

"Lean back against me. Try to give me some of it."

"Thanks."

"Just shake it out. Cry it out. Whatever you gotta do."

No tears fell. No sobs shook his big body. Yet Jav knew Stef was crying at a cellular level. An upset so deep and elemental, it wouldn't budge. You couldn't force it, like you could force yourself to puke. Putting a finger down the throat of this pain, you'd find no gag reflex. It just sat in your guts and festered.

"Sometimes I make the mistake of thinking I've seen everything," Stef said. "It's an amateur move and it usually ends with me in fetal position on the roof."

"It's okay."

Stef took a few deep breaths, exhaling each one heavier. "I'm kind of loving you right now," he said.

"Same."

A big sigh and Stef melted a little bit more against Jav. His hands came up to twine fingers with Jav and held on tight.

"I need you to know you're everything to me," Jav said. "This. Right here. Means everything to me."

Stef nodded, face squeezed tight. Shivering and hurting and beautiful in Jav's arms.

"You're freezing," Jav said, taking a bit of charge. "Come inside now."

"Yeah, I don't need to die of pneumonia for this."

"Chinese tonight? Beers?"

"Intravenously," Stef said, pulling open the stairwell door. "Lots."

"Sex?"

Stef's laugh echoed off the concrete walls. "I don't know. Let me eat something and get drunk." He stopped on a landing. He didn't turn around but kept both hands on opposite rails, blocking the way. "I'm still loving you."

Jav slid his forearms around Stef's neck and pressed their cold heads together. "Don't stop."

I CAN'T EVEN DO BUT WANT

"WHAT'S WITH YOU TONIGHT, LANDES?"

"I don't know."

Stef lay sprawled on the bed. Arms flung over his head. Huge breaths expanding and contracting his rib cage like bellows, his waist almost fragile beneath. His chest hair slick with sweat. The trail of fine hairs leading down from his belly button drawing up into damp spirals.

"Jesus," Jav whispered.

"What?"

"Just looking at you." Staring, breathing just as hard, Jav set his palms on Stef's sides, holding him above the hips. His knees were open to the sides and Jav could see everything. All of him. Every vulnerable private part naked and blatant and exposed.

I want all of this. I need to have all of this. I want to suck him with my mouth, lick him with my tongue, touch him with my fingers and fuck him with my cock. I'm not afraid or grossed out by anything his body does. If he comes on me, drools on me, sweats on me or gets his shit on me, I don't care.

I don't fucking care.

I want all of this.

I want all of him. I want him on his back, on his stomach, on his knees. I want in his mouth and in his hands and in his ass until I fucking die.

"Dude, when you look at me like that?" Stef whispered. "I swear I'm gonna lose my mind."

"I swear I don't know what to do with you sometimes." Jav fell onto his palms. Stef caught his kiss, fingers digging tight in Jav's hair, turning his head this way and that.

"Here's what's you'll do," he said. "First, you're gonna get me ready. Then, you're gonna fuck me the way you look at me."

Jav crawled backward along Stef's body, kissing and licking down his chest and stomach and then pulling him into his mouth. His hands pushed Stef's legs wide, thumbs sliding into the crack of his ass and pulling him apart, spreading him open. Touching and tasting every fold and ridge and crevice. Drunk on it. Crazed by it. Consumed with needing to make Stef come to him.

And stay.

"Last," Stef said. "Don't stop. Whatever you got going on tonight, whatever's in your head, whatever's driving you to be like this... Don't even think about stopping."

"I can't," Jav said. He rolled Stef over. Stuffed pillows under his stomach to get his hips up high so Jav could suck and lick him from behind. He danced on the edge of a dire insanity. No matter what side, direction or angle he came at Stef, he couldn't get enough.

Stef's voice floated over the desperation. "Don't. Fucking. Stop."

Dragging a forearm across his mouth, Jav got up on his knees. His hands slipped and slid as he poured more lube on them and worked it in. His hands shook as he lined up the head of his cock and pushed it into Stef's ass.

"Slow," Stef said, drawing the word out long. "Give it to me slow."

Jav shut his eyes and drew the intensity inward, wrapping it around them like golden cords. They stretched in all directions, keeping tension on him, holding him suspended. He leaned into their resistance as he moved his hips forward, taking Stef inch by inch.

He's taking me, he thought. *He can take me. He's the only one who can.*

"Nobody," he said, running his hands up and down Stef's tattooed back. "Nobody will ever do to me what you do. Nobody will ever make me feel this way."

Stef put one hand, then the other on the headboard, pulling himself upright. His palms slid flat on the wall, the inked wings on his shoulders spreading wide. Jav slid arms around him, one hand flat on his heart, the other closing around his cock. His mouth dragged up the side of Stef's neck, tangy and salty with sweat. Stef shivered. His body trembled as he sat back on Jav, coming down in his lap and taking all of him inside.

"Don't move," he said thickly, lacing his hands behind his head.

"I can feel your heartbeat."

"I can't feel anything but you."

Jav turned Stef's chin back, curled around and kissed him. Bit gently on his lips and sucked his tongue and inhaled the ragged exhales. Pressing Stef between his arm and his body, holding him tight, holding him still and stroking him off. When he took his mouth away, Stef's head lolled like his neck had no strength left. His hands reached for the wall again.

"So fucking deep," he whispered down between his arms. A groaning, babbling sing-song of words as Jav moved in him. Slurred run-on sentences pouring out of his soul. "God Jav you're so full up tight deep in my ass all the time I can't even do but want you fucking into me like this..."

"I want to make you come."

"Fuck into me like this."

"Come here, Stef. Come right now."

"Jav, I can't even..."

"Do what I tell you." He drew Stef's head back and covered his mouth with his own. "*Come*," he said into Stef's throat.

Stef moved on him, short little thrusts while his hand wrapped around Jav's and jerked hard. His cry echoed off the insides of Jav's mouth before his head fell forward, then back. His moan bounced off the walls and ceiling. Cock bubbling up hot and dripping through their hands. Ass clenching down even hotter, pulsing as Jav held still and came into pieces.

"Javi," Stef whispered. Beads of sweat slid down his temple. "I swear..."

"I know, man. Hang onto me. Come down now." Holding Stef to him with one arm, he put the other hand down and rolled them onto their sides, carefully easing out of Stef's twitching body. Stef made a little grunt and then shivered into stillness.

"So good," he said, the words slurred and mushy. "Nobody in my life ever fucked me like that."

"Nobody ever will." Jav wrapped arms around him, burying his mouth against Stef's hot, damp head a minute. "I'll get a towel."

"Not yet, stay here."

Jav settled back down, pulling him close.

"Just hold onto me a minute," Stef whispered. The twitching aftershocks had blended into a definitive rumble in his limbs.

"Cold?" Jav asked.

"Yeah, I got chilled off. Like all my body heat left when I came like that."

Jav drew the covers up over them and tucked them tight. "There."

"Fuck, that was intense."

"I know."

"Need to come down."

"I got you."

"Weird," Stef said, his teeth chattering. His skin rose up in bumps. His limbs trembled. Then, fast as it had come over him, it left. His body softened, his breathing quieted until it fell beneath silence. Long, rolling inhales and exhales, like ocean waves.

"I love making love with you," Jav whispered, the words tiny and shy in his mouth.

No answer.

"You all right?"

The finch was asleep in his arms. Still glistening with sweat. A tiny smile holding his mouth in a curve.

Jav rested his forehead on Stef's nape, smiling as well.

All is right.

TELL ME

STEF AWOKE THE NEXT MORNING, hard and twitchy. His head full of tender thoughts while his body only wanted to fuck.

Can't it be both?

Jav was asleep on his stomach, his head turned away and his fingers lightly twined with Stef.

Wake up and look at me.

Jav was so intense and private about his sleep. He could only be spooned so long before he inched away, turned over on his stomach and put his back to the world so he could put the day away.

He shared Stef's bed yet he slept alone.

But he liked to hold hands through the night. Even turned away, he reached back and behind to find Stef's fingers.

Do you need me?

Stef reached to caress him, then stopped and only let his palm hover a quarter-inch above Jav's skin. Moving atop the force field. Almost touching.

Wanting so bad it hurt.

Tell me, he imagined Jav saying. *I won't laugh.*

One day, Stef's mouth moved around silent words. *Someday. I'm going to fuck you.*

How, Jav said, his fingers tightening.

I'm going to kiss you until you're limp. Then turn you away and bend you over my bed. Then I'll slowly pull your pants down and lick you in places you didn't know you wanted my tongue to touch. Then I'll roll you over and wrap my mouth around your cock and slide my fingers into your ass. One at a time I'll work them into you. I don't care if it takes an hour to get you to open. Get you loose. Get you begging for me to fill you up because you need to be close to me.

God, I want to hear you say you need me in you. I'll make it so good, Jav, I swear. I'll hold your trust tight in my hands like it's the best gift I've ever been given. I'll get you so ready and slowly, watching your face the whole time, I'll slide my cock into you. Wrap you in my fist while I breach that tight, hot ass of yours.

I don't want to scare you. I don't want to make you something you're not. If it takes months, it takes months. If it's never, it's never. But if you want it...

His chest got thick and muddy, desire caressing the back of his throat like a waft of perfume.

If you want it, Jav, if you want me in you, then we'll go slow. Slow as you want. Kill an entire bottle of lube if we have to. Just the tip until I feel you relax for me, feel you start to want me. Want more. A quarter inch at a time I'll fuck into you. Until you have all of me and you're fucking my hand while I'm fucking your sweet ass. I'll make you come harder than you ever came in your life, Jav. You'll be dying for my cock after that. You'll want me to fuck you all the time. And I will. Anytime you want. Anytime you ask me. Anytime you tell me.

His palm touched down, spread wide and warm on Jav's back.

And each time I'll be wondering if you have any idea how crazy about you I am. If you know I've never wanted anyone, male or female, the way I want you. That I'm just as shocked as you to hear this kind of stuff coming out of my mouth. I've never talked like this to anyone. I've never wanted to say these kinds of things to anyone. Never felt this way with anyone else.

Every time I fuck you, I'll be wondering if you know what all of this means to me...

Jav rolled over, the sheets twisting around his body. "I can hear you thinking, you know."

"Come here, you moron."

Jav yawned, then pushed his face into Stef's side and his arm slid heavy and warm across Stef's stomach.

"Tell me more," he said.

ONE FOR THE ROAD

I never had any intention of this scene being in the final draft. Jav would never want to work again and Stef would never let him. —SLQR

"I NEED TO TALK to you about something," Jav said.

"Oh boy." Stef closed his laptop. "Well, we knew we'd get to this point someday. Honeymoon's over."

"Whenever you're done."

"Sorry. What's up?"

"I got an email from one of my clients. She was a regular of mine for years. She needs a date and she begged me to walk her."

"What did you tell her?"

"Nothing yet, I wanted to talk to you about it."

"You're asking my permission?"

"No," Jav said slowly. "Yes. Kind of."

Stef scratched fingers along Roman's head. "Well, when you say *date*, is that a biblical date?"

"It could be. Or it could be just a walk. I haven't talked to her about the specifics yet."

Stef crossed his arms and his ankles. "We got tested but we really haven't talked about exclusivity."

Jav nodded. "Do you want to?"

"Be exclusive?"

"I'm not sleeping with anyone else."

"Neither am I."

Roman looked from one man to the other, not sure what had been decided or declared.

"At this moment," Jav said. "I don't want to sleep with anyone else."

"Me neither."

Roman yawned.

"Glad we had this little chat," Stef said, trying to focus on the point but the sun was coming in the windows and backlighting Jav's neck and shoulders. He wore jeans and a grey thermal shirt. His clothes clung to some of his muscles and left no doubt, and draped in other places, making Stef imagine things.

"If you're only walking her, I guess it's okay," he said.

"I was thinking I'd do it for free."

Stef chewed on that and found, oddly, the money being out of the picture made the scenario *not* okay. "This is weird," he said, "but I almost rather you do it as a job."

"Huh."

"And only as a walk. I mean, I'm not laying out a command here. I'm just saying how I feel."

"No, go on with the command thing. It's hot."

Stef threw a pillow at him. Laughing, Jav caught it.

"I'm serious," he said. "Lay out the rules."

"The rules?"

"Put it on the table."

"All right. Number one, you tell her you're seeing someone."

"Done."

"And it's a walk. No sex."

"No sex."

"And no kissing."

"No kissing."

"I mean, you can kiss her on the cheek..."

"No tongue."

"Right." Stef caught the pillow Jav flung back and hugged it to his chest. "I wait here for you."

"I like that rule. What happens when I get home?"

"You hand over the money and I fuck you senseless."

A crackling moment of smiling silence.

"You whore," Jav said.

Stef opened his laptop. "Oh, you have no idea..."

HE WASN'T WORRIED. But he ambushed Jav in the shower and jerked him off anyway. "Just to empty the tank," he said.

"Great, now I'm sleepy," Jav said from under the spray.

"Which means you'll be home even earlier."

Stef almost changed his mind when he saw Jav emerge from the bedroom in suit and tie, his trench coat over an arm.

Holy fuck. "You look like shit," he said.

"Thank you."

"Goddamn, Landes, you scrub up nice."

"Stop staring at my ass," Jav said.

"Impossible."

"I'll text you when I'm leaving."

"Nah. Just show up and surprise me."

"Whatever you want." Gazing in the mirror by the door, Jav gave his tie a little adjustment and pulled on his cuffs.

"You look good," Stef said.

"Thank you."

"You wearing underwear?"

"Yes, dear."

"Got condoms in your wallet?"

Jav opened his mouth then shut it, eyebrows drawing down. He took out his wallet and opened it, then chuckled and tossed two Trojans to Stef. "There you go. I'm unarmed and dangerous."

"I'm kidding, I'm kidding." He made to toss them back but Jav put up a shooing hand, then leaned and kissed him. "I'll be back."

"Well, you live here."

Jav kissed him again. "Make yourself at home."

Stef did. And truthfully, he was tired, and it was nice to have a night in. Nice to be sprawled on the couch, watching TV, with Roman and all of Jav's things for company. He made a little dinner and cleaned up. Took Roman for a last walk. Every now and then he glanced at his watch and wondered what Jav was doing, but with a benign curiosity. He wasn't worried.

It was nearing one in the morning when Jav's key scraped in the lock.

"Honey, I'm home," he called softly as Roman trotted over, dog tags jingling.

"How was your day, dear?"

"Fine."

Jav looked tired. A slightly blurred version of the sleek, sharp man who'd left the apartment five hours before. He looked gorgeous. But he looked forty-five, too.

"Have a good time?" Stef asked.

"It's a job," Jav said. "It's not about me having a good time."

"Must be exhausting," Stef said. "Keeping your attention focused on someone that intensely for that long."

"It can be." Jav had shed his trench and suit jacket and was pouring rum into a lowball. It was the only hard liquor he drank. And always Appleton Estate. Stef didn't care for it, although he liked the taste of it when they were kissing.

Jav sat on his desk chair, loosening his tie and undoing a couple buttons on his dress shirt. As they talked, he took out his cufflinks and rolled his sleeves up. It made for a pleasing picture. Something vintage 1950s about it, Stef thought, his eyes narrowing. Frank Sinatra after a gig in Vegas. One for my baby and one more for the road.

"What?" Jav said.

"Nothing."

"What?"

"Just... You look fucking hot right now and I'm not really listening."

Jav smiled into his glass. "My conversation is shit, but I scrub up nice sometimes."

The room expanded and contracted like a pair of lungs as the two men stared.

"You know, I'm kind of falling for you," Stef said.

Jav's chin raised and lowered. "You know, I couldn't wait to get home."

Stef got up and crossed to the desk. Ran fingertips along Jav's neck and touched the hollow at the base of his throat. Let them trail down Jav's chest, feeling his skin rise up in tiny bumps.

"Put that down," Stef said, indicating the lowball glass.

Jav chugged the rest and set the glass on the desk. The heady smell of rum mixed with the even headier scent of Jav's skin, hair and clothes. Stef was getting drunker by the minute. His hand caressed along the open buttons of Jav's shirt and began undoing the closed ones.

"Tell me about your date."

"What do you want to know?"

"Was she hot?"

"Yeah." Jav drew in a small breath as Stef pulled the shirt tails from the waistband so he could get the last button.

"She turn you on?"

"No."

His fingers parted the shirt lapels and glided over Jav's stomach and chest. "Does this?"

Jav nodded.

Stef set his hands on top of Jav's on the armrests. Slowly he leaned, tilting the chair back.

"Do I?"

Jav wet his lips. "Couldn't wait to get home."

Stef smiled at him, then leaned further and settled his mouth on Jav's neck, gently sucking at the warm, tender skin of his throat. Jav pulled in another breath, this one gruff and ragged in his chest. He sighed as Stef ran his lips along collarbones and the underside of Jav's jaw.

"Finch, kiss me," Jav said hoarsely.

Stef took his head. No soft, slow buildup tonight. Jav's mouth was open right away and pulling Stef's tongue inside.

"I don't want anyone else but you," Jav whispered.

"Good."

"Now that I know what making love is really like, I never want to work again."

"I don't want you to either," Stef said. "I'm getting really greedy." He went after Jav's mouth again, a hand tight in his hair, trying to swallow the man alive.

"I've never felt like this," Jav said. "Never in my life. This is more feeling than I ever had in my life."

"Me too." Stef held Jav's head, smoothing a thumb over that full bottom lip. "My heart's pounding."

"You know you have more of me than anyone else ever has."

"I know. I'll be really careful with it."

"Promise?"

Stef held his lips against Jav's, breathing. "It's safe with me."

"Finch." Jav's hands came up to hold his head. "I swear to God, I'm in love with you."

The whole room contracted like a fist, then released.

"I'm in love with you, too," Stef whispered.

"Want you so bad."

"I want to make you come."

"Let's go in the other room."

"No," Stef said, crouching down. "I ruined one profession. If I suck you off at your desk, maybe I can ruin the other one, too."

Jav laughed. "I'll be useless."

"I have tremendous use for you." Stef undid Jav's belt buckle. "Watch." Shaking fingers unbuttoned and unzipped. Jav's legs flexed and he pushed up, freeing his hips, letting Stef slide his pants and briefs down. He sprawled in the office chair like an executive god. Shirt unbuttoned, tie undone, pants around his ankles and a hand closing around his erection, his thumb rolling in a slow circle around the tip. Breathing hard and staring down at Stef on his knees.

"I love looking at you."

"I love you looking at me." Stef slid his hands up Jav's strong quads, slowly bringing them in to frame the base of his cock. "This mine?"

"Mm," Jav said.

"All for me?"

"All of it." Jav's free hand slid around the back of Stef's head, fingers folding into his hair, bringing him closer. Stef closed his eyes and let Jav guide and slide into his mouth.

"*Christ*," Jav moaned.

Stef laughed around his cock, slowly released him and ran his tongue around the ridge. "Glad you're home."

Jav's fingers tightened, something between a snarl and a growl in his throat. "Been fucking dying for your mouth all night."

Stef's erection screamed from inside his pants, begging to be let out. He gave his crotch a single, adjusting squeeze, telling it to cut the shit. "Oh yeah?"

"Take it," Jav said, rocking his hips. "Please, man. Want it so fucking bad."

Stef made short work of him. Within minutes Jav let out a yell and blew his load on Stef's tongue, his heels digging into the floor and fingers clenched white on the armrests. Stef caught his breath, then, still kneeling, he eased off Jav's shoes and socks, pulled his pants the rest of the way off. Reached up and helped his arms out of his shirt sleeves.

"Come here," he said, standing up and pulling Jav's naked body against his fully-clothed one. "Listen to me."

"What?"

Stef held Jav's head and told him, "Tonight was your last job."

A beat of staring silence before Jav whispered, "All right."

"You're no longer for sale," Stef said. "Nobody ever pays for you again. Not for your body, not even for your time."

"You get my time now," Jav said. "And my body. You get all of me."

Another fragile beat before each eased into the other's arms. Skin against cloth. Stef slid his hand along the back of Jav's neck, staring with an intense ferocity at the room and the world. Mouth moving around silent words.

You are no longer for sale, Javier Landes.

BABBLING IN THAT WEIRD LANGUAGE

"DUDE, THAT WASN'T EVEN ENGLISH," Jav said.

A forearm flung over his face, Stef babbled something, giggling, his toes still clenched up tight.

"Pardon?" Jav said.

"I said, I'll get you for this."

And later, he did.

"Christ, I love your mouth," Jav said to the ceiling.

"Mm."

He pushed up on his elbows to watch.

I'm watching a guy blow me.

And it is fucking hot.

"Want something inside?"

Jav licked his lips, swallowed hard. "Yeah."

Stef pulled off the rings he wore on his index and middle fingers. "Hold these for me."

"Oh God," Jav whispered. He lay down again, one damp palm curling around the bits of silver, the other reaching to rest on Stef's head.

"We'll go slow." Stef flipped the cap of the lube up. "I'll stop whenever you want."

He gently nudged one of Jav's knees up. Then he took Jav's hand off his head and held it on the mattress. Jav focused on the feel of their palms resting together. The fit of their fingers. The warm wet engulfing his cock again as a slick caress started stroking along his ass.

"Don't hold your breath," Stef said, licking along the ridge.

Jav exhaled.

It was most intense at the first breach. When the involuntary urge was to clench. Jav remembered to breathe out as the pressure moved in.

"Hurt?" Stef murmured.

"No." It burned a little at first. On its own, it was weird. But together with Stef's mouth it was amazing. And when his finger moved a little deeper and found that golden spot of tickling, tingling, pulsing joy, it was fucking *crazy.*

And tonight, it kind of wasn't enough.

"That just one?" he said through his teeth.

"Mm."

"Maybe...try another."

The cool drip of more lube and then the sensation was doubled. Stef moved his mouth slow along Jav's hardness, holding them poised on an agonizing edge.

It wasn't enough.

"Try," Jav said, his eyes squeezed shut. "More."

Stef's fingers pressed deeper, dragging along Jav's prostate as they slid back out. The tingling intensified until it spread from Jav's earlobes to the soles of his feet.

"There?" Stef said, kneading in a little circle.

"There," Jav gasped, seeing stars. This was the need center of his existence. Every nerve trembling and howling with *need need need need.* Screaming in frustration when Stef's hand pulled back and held still, just the tips inside, hanging Jav by the moment.

"More," Jav gasped. "Don't fucking stop, man."

"You want more then take it," Stef said. His mouth came gliding up Jav's stomach and chest, sucking and biting. Fingers tight in Jav's hair and pulling Jav's groaning panting mouth against his cool smile. "Go on. Fuck my fingers. Get off on it. Make yourself come."

Jav hesitated. He hadn't quite yet given himself permission to actively want this. To go get it for himself.

"Go on," Stef said softly. "You can."

And, as he thought so many other times in bed with Stef, Jav thought now, *Oh fuck it.*

He drove down on Stef's wrist, filling himself up. Sliding and clenching and taking more and more. He reached for his cock with one hand and the lube with the other and then he was sprawled in the sheets, wide open and writhing. Hips bucking up into his slippery fist and down onto Stef's slick fingers, fucking himself. Openly and unabashedly masturbating in front of this guy who stared down at him, transfixed, lips parted and eyes wide, like he was watching the creation of the universe.

"God, you are so fucking hot," he whispered. He set his palm on Jav's sternum and pressed him down into the bed. His fingers beckoned, curling around that narthex of pleasure. It vibrated so deep, Jav couldn't even pinpoint where it stopped and his own hand began.

"There," Jav said through his teeth. "Right there. Right there don't stop. Jesus Stef don't stop..." And then it was his speech that slid out of English, past Spanish and into some ancient primitive tongue. It was him lying spent and giggling afterward, toes curled and limbs tingling. Stef wiping him off and laughing softly, too.

"I think we're inventing a new language, Landes."

The cloth moved gently, picking up the residue of spit and lube and semen. Jav closed his eyes under the touch. He found he was starting to adore those little moments of caring afterglow as much as he did the sex. When Stef dried him off and then got a bottle of water. Asked if he was okay or if he needed anything. Blithe and unconscious kindness. The *tending* to. Someone giving a damn about Jav for once. A couple times it left him on the verge of tears, which he hid by lying on his stomach, head turned away while Stef's palm stroked up and down his back.

"This is big," Stef said. "This is just more than I ever..."

"Yeah," Jav whispered. "I know."

Be brave, he told himself. *Eres el más valiente.*

He turned his head and let Stef see the enormity brimming his eyes. Stef gazed back. His hand dropped softly on Jav's face. He didn't speak. Just held Jav's gaze as his thumb ran along Jav's cheekbone or along his eyebrow.

"It's amazing," Jav said, giving a little shiver. "Everything I thought about being a man is...not what I thought."

Stef nodded. His hand reached down to draw up the covers. "This is gonna sound strange," he said. "But I don't think I've ever felt more like a man in my life. I can't even say why."

"I feel like me."

The corner of Stef's mouth lifted in a tired smile. "I feel like I finally met someone who literally speaks my language."

The new vocabulary grew bolder and bigger on Jav's tongue. He relaxed into the syntax and structure, realizing that "having sex" could mean a number of different things and as Stef said, the things didn't always involve someone's ass. Sometimes the things were nothing more than a straight-forward hand job because it was a crummy Tuesday night after a long hard day of work, they were tired, they both wanted to blow a load and go the fuck to sleep. Business was brisk. They could make each other come in two minutes. Tops. Breath was caught, a hand towel passed from one to the other, boxers and sweats pulled back on and 'night, dude.

Sometimes a Tuesday stretched out long and naked, glazed in sweat and juice, until it reached into the wee hours of Wednesday. Leaving both of them stumbling around their work, guzzling coffee and talking through yawns, texting each other sheepishly that fucking all night *seemed* a good idea at the time. But really they were a little old for these shenanigans. They'd cool it after midnight next time. And then next time came and suddenly it was four in the morning and they were babbling in that weird language again, unable to stop.

"I can't get enough," Stef said hoarsely. "Jesus Christ, dude, your sex is like voodoo or some shit."

Jav didn't answer, his mouth caught between kissing Stef and trying to swallow him.

Inside, he thought, dire and desperate. *This is what it's like wanting someone inside you.*

I WAS FIVE WHEN YOU WERE BORN

"CHECK IT OUT." Stef's expression was full of the devil as he elbowed Jav's side.

Jav looked over, annoyed that the liquor store was out of Appleton Estate and he had to pick another kind of rum. He took off his glasses and squinted at the shelf where Stef was pointing to a bag's label.

Rimming Sugar.

Sweet Cocktail Trim.

"Man, I would've loved being in that advertising meeting," Stef said, grinning.

"Jesus," Jav said. "Were they even trying to be subliminal?"

"Hidden in plain sight."

As Jav went back to inspecting rum labels, a small elephant tugged on his sleeve.

Shut up, he thought.

Dumbo pouted. *But we wants to know.*

"Now see," Stef said, picking up another bag. "This is poor advertising." He turned it toward Jav. The label read *Chocolate Rimming Sugar.* "Two words you definitely don't want next to each other. Probably doesn't sell very well."

The elephant was beating Jav with its trunk now. *We wants to know!*

"You ever?" Jav said, circling his hand vaguely at the shelves.

"Sure."

"Rimmer or rimmee?"

"Both."

"Which do you like better?"

Stef put the bag back on the shelf. "Both."

Jav blinked. Trying, unsuccessfully, to get the picture in his mind. Knowing he'd left the words "I'll never" in the dust months ago.

"Well, I don't doubt we'll be having those drinks someday," he said.

"You save it for date four hundred and seventy-two." Stef smiled and moved a few aisles over toward the bourbons. Jav's eyes followed, full of confused affection. He knew beer would always be Stef's best friend. He liked IPAs in summer but when autumn rolled around, he started drinking heavier, darker brews. Porters and stouts. In real cold weather, he liked a lowball of bourbon. He especially favored a brand called High West Yippee Ki-Yay. Probably because the label had a picture of a cowboy riding a bucking bronco. Stef favored anything with a picture of a horse on it.

Jav knew things like this now.

He grudgingly took a bottle of Pusser's rum and made his way to the line at the register. From his pocket, his phone pinged an incoming text. He fished it out. It was Stef.

FYI, more nerve endings in your anus than any other part of your body.

Laughter snorted through Jav's nose as a fiery heat swept across his face. "Jesus Christ," he muttered, pulled in all direction by happiness, squeamishness, arousal and trepidation. Sloshing together in his stomach and groin in a passionate but lethal cocktail. Rimmed with sugar.

He had an erection now.

What the fuck is happening to me?

"GOD, MY NECK," Jav said, moaning.

"Get off the fucking computer already." Stef hooked arms around Jav from behind and bit his ear. "Come on. I want to show you a great documentary on wild ass."

"Oh? The ones that roam your mattress?"

"Them. Come on. Let me rub your back and graze on your plains."

"Maybe you should write this book."

"Me do the words good." Stef reached and turned the desk lamp off. "Get the fuck in my bed, Landes."

"I'm starting to think you have an agenda."

"I do."

"Should I shower? Is this under-the-sink agenda?"

"If you want," Stef said, swirling his bourbon glass and tapping his finger on the rim.

Jav crossed his arms, biting down on a corner of his smile. "Real subtle, Finch."

"So's your curiosity. I can taste it from here."

"Shut up."

"It's like chocolate rimming sugar."

Jav sighed, shaking his head. Red-faced and sporting a half-chubber, he headed for the bathroom.

"Yippee Ki-Yay, motherfucker," Stef called after him.

He half-expected to walk into the bedroom and find it lit up with candles, Stef lounging naked in the center of the bed with a rose in his teeth. But he knew better. Stef detested cheesy, staged seduction scenes. He always left the jokes and wisecrack remarks in the living room. He lay soft and chill on his side of the bed, wearing sweats and a T-shirt, reading under his bedside table lamp. Only one candle was lit on his corner altar.

Jav put on his own sweats and lay down on his stomach. Stef dropped a hand on the back of his neck and kneaded it.

"Ow," Jav sighed.

"Occupational hazard."

"Yeah."

A few moments of page-turning quiet, then Stef set his book down and turned the lamp off.

It started fine, with him kneeling astride the small of Jav's back and his huge hands wringing the knots out of Jav's neck and shoulders. It got great when Stef started biting on Jav's nape, digging fingers into his hair and pulling a little. Then kissing down Jav's spine and running his tongue along the edges of Jav's shoulder blades. His nose slid along the waistband of Jav's sweats, his fingers curled and slowly dragged them down.

Goosebumps rashed Jav's skin and his groin rolled over like a cat belly-up in the sun. Someday, he'd tell Stef that the only reason he wore sweats or shorts to bed was so Stef could take them off.

You mean pull them down.

His chest got all thick and tight. Once, just once, when they were making out hot and heavy and Stef was letting Jav suck on his fingers in between feverish kissing, he leaned his face into Jav's neck and whispered, "Pull your pants down."

Jav almost died.

Died as in he was instantly hard, filled with the *Oh shit* of intense arousal and the *Oh shit* of being in big trouble.

Pull your pants down.

A million connotations packed into four words. Your adult self hoping you were getting fucked while your inner child thought it was getting a beating. You didn't know if you were facing heaven or humiliation.

Well, your brain knew. Your ass wasn't so sure. And it was fucking hot. Strange, but hot. It stuck in Jav's spank bank like a golden go-to. All he had to do was think about Stef whispering the words. Or think about him unbuttoning and unzipping Jav's jeans and starting to pull them...

Christ, I'm weird, he thought, happily dying as Stef slid his pants off and ran his big hands up Jav's legs.

It was good. It all felt good. It was literally all right until Stef slid a hand on either side of Jav's ass and slowly spread him apart. One ruffle of Stef's breath on the back side of his business and something felt all wrong. Inherently, almost culturally wrong.

Jav willed himself to relax, even as the goosebumps rushed in waves over his skin again and a dreadful anticipation folded the sides of his stomach together. Everything in him screamed to laugh it off, make a joke. It was one thing to have a guy check out your ass from across the room. Another for him to be up close, peeking through your back door window. Like it was something remotely desirable.

He's right, Jav thought. *There's no sexy language for this. Only fifth-*

grade jokes.

Stef laughed softly. "I can hear you thinking, you know."

"Well, I talk out my ass a lot. You're in the prime place to overhear."

Stef gave him a small shove, still chuckling. "Maybe we'll do this some other time."

"No, I... I just need to get used to it. This is the self-conscious weirdness of a guy looking at my asshole. It's not making me hard at the moment, it's making me...dumb. Give me a minute."

Stef sighed. "No good words."

"I'm sorry."

"Jav, if you apologize I'm going to punch you."

"All right, I'm s... Never mind."

"Let's just not talk, okay? Put some music on, put your clothes back on, I'll leave your ass alone."

Jav batted away the sweats Stef threw at his head. *He's frustrated as shit with me*, he thought. *God, I'm such a fucking dork.*

"Quit brooding and put on that Feist album you were playing the other day," Stef said. "It was cool."

Biting his tongue nearly to the breaking point, Jav put it on and forced himself to lay down and shut up. He curled arms around a pillow and exhaled. Stef stretched out beside him, head pillowed in the small of Jav's back.

Just lie here. Be naked. Be present. And fucking chill.

One of Stef's hands moved over his skin, warm and neutral. Massaging his muscles. Fingertips finding the fine hairs at the base of Jav's spine and combing his nails through them. His palm ran in circles on Jav's butt, his thumb digging into the meaty part sore from yesterday's workout. Then it planed along Jav's spine to find the howling tension at the base of his skull.

Stef clicked his tongue, fingers pressing. "God, you're a wreck."

Jav grunted. Editing took a toll on his entire body. Brain. Bones. Muscles. All of him clenched like a fist while he tried to get it right.

"Jesus," he said as Stef's fingers dug into one of the more stubborn knots and the pain rocketed up the side of Jav's face.

"Sorry."

"No, it feels good," Jav murmured. He'd drooled a little against the pillowcase.

"You work hard," Stef said.

"Not as hard as you."

"It's different work. And I couldn't do it."

Jav moved one leg over a little and let his breath out. Dialed into the feel of the fleece sheets on his bare skin, Stef's warm strong hand caressing him. The music. The flicker of the candle on Stef's shrine. A curl of incense smoke rising up in front of the statue of Kwon Yin. This room a shrine of its own. An oasis of privacy and vulnerability and trust.

Trust him, he thought.

I want to. I trust him. I just don't trust...this. I don't yet trust in its permanence. I keep waiting to find out it can't be mine.

And what if it turns out not to be yours? Will avoiding something tonight be some kind of consolation later? Wow, thank God I didn't let him eat my ass that night, I'd feel so much worse. I sure dodged that bullet.

He sighed. *No good words.*

Stef sighed too, his breath warm. "Now what are you thinking?"

Jav turned his head on the pillow to look at him. "That I really do trust you. More than anyone I ever trusted in my life."

Stef was drawing up and down in the hollows between Jav's ribs. "I'm glad I met you now."

"What do you mean?"

"If you were twenty-five and saying something like that, I'd just kind of shake my head and indulge it, knowing you were too young to know what a lifetime meant. But saying it now? Four decades is a good long time to know a few things about yourself. So it means something. It means more than sex. It fucking means the world."

Stef went quiet as Feist started singing "The Limit to Your Love." His hand running in long strokes along Jav's leg, thumb caressing the inside of his thigh and along the curve of one cheek.

Jav moved his legs apart a little more. Stef's hand slid along his quadriceps, curled under his knee and gently nudged it to bend up and out. "Let me look at you," he whispered. "Trust that I want to."

Jav relaxed his fingers. He realized he was starting to want it, too, and as he moved his leg, he shifted to get his stiffening cock into a more comfortable place.

He felt Stef sit up on an elbow. His fingertips moved closer. The pad of his thumb brushing the quivering, sensitive entrance then moving away again. Coming back. Then his mouth glided across Jav's lower back. A trail of hard kisses, interspersed with the gentle bite of his teeth. The softness of his mouth within the rough of his beard growth. The wide, warm span of his palm. The stroke of his fingertips. The tiny scratch of short nails. The silken wet of his tongue inching toward where it shouldn't go, and yet...

"God," Jav cried out, seized with a desire to both pull away and push into it. It was too much. Too intimate. Too intense. Too fraught with nerves wired against intrusion. Yet as soon as Stef's mouth moved away, Jav wanted it again.

"Come back," he said.

Stef slid between Jav's sprawled legs. His fingers spread Jav wide open and then his tongue, God his fucking tongue. Jav moaned at first, then howled out loud as Stef wormed a hand between the mattress and Jav's body and took hold of Jav's cock, rock hard and screaming now. Stef squeezed and stroked as his mouth kissed and his tongue licked.

"Come," he said. "If it feels good, then fuck my hand hard and come."

Jav hesitated a last split second before toppling over the edge of himself. Spread wide and wanton, his hips bucking up to give Stef's hand more room to slide and jerk. Give Stef's mouth more room to get in close, get in tight, go down and get his damn *tongue* in where Jav was dying for it now. Thick pleasure wrestling with some animalistic need he didn't know existed in him, but now it was woken like a bear and roaring to be filled. His groin clenched, reared up like an angry stallion, hooves kicking at the air.

"Come for me," Stef said, his mouth slick and dripping. "Come in my hand now."

Jav exploded with a yell, pinwheeling through the sky in a free-falling dive. Plummeting through crystallized blue and white, not caring how or where he landed because Stef would catch him.

All my life, he thought, the sky slipping through his fingers. *Where have I been all my life?*

"Finch," he cried, his voice cracking open.

Where were you? How did I not know? How did I live so long not knowing where you were?

"Finch..."

I was five when you were born. How did I even live for five years without you existing somewhere in the world?

His teeth curled over his bottom lip, trying to form another "Finch" and failing. Just a weak exhaled "fuh" before his body shivered into stillness.

"Jesus," Stef whispered, elbowing his way up the mattress.

"I've never come like that," Jav said.

Stef wrapped arms around him from behind, pulling Jav against his chest.

"I've never known anything like it in my life," Jav said, near desperation.

My life, Stef. My life. You don't know, you don't understand, you have no idea what this is.

Stef buried his face in Jav's hair and held him tight, stilling Jav's shaking limbs. "Me neither."

Jav laughed through a trembling jaw. "Look at me, this is crazy."

Stef held out a hand to show how it shook. "Look at me."

"I can't get you close enough to me. I can't... I can't believe this is happening."

He was caught up tight. One of Stef's arms around his head, the other around his chest. Stef's calf hooked around his legs. All that warm, solid strength snug against Jav's back, coiled around him like a python, squeezing him into place. Holding him fixed in the universe.

I want for nothing right now. Don't let it end. I waited so long. Now just let the rest of my life be this.

WE WANTS IT

STEF SAT ON THE KITCHEN COUNTER, the work day not entirely off his skin yet. Drinking a beer and alternating staring into space with watching Jav cook dinner.

"Who taught you to cook?" he finally asked.

"No one, really. Taught myself."

"But your dad owned a restaurant."

Jav shrugged.

"Did you help out in the kitchen?"

"I washed dishes and made deliveries. Every now and then I'd chop onions or peel plantains. I watched. I had an idea how certain things were made, but I had no use for it, I guess. Not until I left home and realized I couldn't take eating for granted."

"Where did you live?"

"At a teacher's house for a couple months." Jav looked up at the stove hood, wooden spoon poised in the air. "Mr. Durante. Jesus, I wonder if he's still alive. I should find out." He shook his head abruptly. "Anyway, he and his wife fed me. Then that fell through and I slept in a stock room until I finished high school."

"Stock room?"

"Yeah. Neighborhood lady who owned a beauty supply shop. I worked for her unloading boxes. She let me sleep with the inventory. If she was feeling nice she gave me dinner. If she was feeling really nice, I got laid."

"Dinner and a movie."

"Then I rented a room up in Washington Heights. I had access to the kitchen but never had anything to cook with. I ate at the restaurant where I worked. Found a few local places where I could eat cheap. Or free, depending on whether the waitresses liked me."

The last swallow of beer was bitter in Stef's mouth. Sometimes, hearing stories about Jav's early adulthood made him a little miserable. Knowing how sex had turned to currency at such a young age.

I wish I'd known. My family would've taken you in. I could've been your friend. We could've gone through life together...

"Finally, when I got my own place," Jav was saying, "I had to figure out how to eat. So I dredged up memories. I asked the chef at the restaurant. He taught me how to make a steak in a cast-iron pan. Of course, most of the time, I couldn't afford steak."

"Rice and beans."

"Lot of that. Lot of pasta. I kind of messed around and figured out five or six dishes I could rely on. But face it, when I was escorting regularly, I rarely had to make myself dinner."

"Or breakfast," Stef said.

"No, actually, breakfast I made all the time."

"Really? You'd never stay the night?"

Jav shook his head. "Hardly ever."

"Huh. Why?"

Jav's expression was both sad and smug. "Not many women could afford it."

"Ah."

"When I had Ari to take care of, I really had to up the game. Feeding a teenage boy is crazy."

"That'll triple the grocery bill."

"I watched Val Lark cook and she taught me a few things. Plus with the internet these days, if you can read and follow directions, you can cook. And Ari had chops, too. With a single mother, he knew his way around the kitchen. So we did all right."

"How's he doing?"

"He's doing great."

"You miss him?"

"I do. A lot. It's weird."

"Why?"

90

Jav opened the fridge to get two more beers. "All those years not even knowing he existed. It's crazy how quickly I felt... I don't know. Ownership isn't the right word. This sense of him being my blood. He belonged to me. This was my sister-son. It was mindless. And fast. Like it was coded into my DNA and it woke up as soon as my genes smelled his..."

His voice and his eyes trailed off. His face morphed into a look Stef was beginning to recognize.

"You're getting an idea," he said.

Jav didn't look away from horizon of his imagination. "Yeah. Just a..."

Laughing, Stef slid down from the counter and took the wooden spoon. "Go get it. I'll finish this."

Watching Jav scribble feverishly for ten minutes, Stef was equal parts fascination, affection and envy. The envy was sub-divided as well. For all his artistic talent, Stef had never been able to corral words together on paper. He wished he had a fraction of Jav's wordsmithing. But he also harbored a deeper and slightly unattractive jealousy for that notebook and its pages holding Jav's secret thoughts and ideas. Sometimes the mere, innocuous sight of it on the desk or bedside table made Stef's eyes bulge like Gollum's, his fingers itchy and covetous.

We wants it.

Hell if he'd ask to see it. Jav once said if he knew a friend was reading one of his books, he never asked if they finished or what they thought.

"Feedback's no fun when you have to fish for it," he said.

Stef agreed. Same way the blow job given voluntarily was sweeter than the one you had to ask for. And the secrets freely divulged were more precious than the ones you had to coax out like a shy girl at a party, or pull out like rotten teeth. Stef got his fill of coaxing and pulling all day at his job. He wanted to know everything going on in Jav's head, but he'd let it come to him.

Jav straightened up and threw the pen down with an accomplished exhale. He was beautiful. Pleased and exhilarated and smug.

"Get it?" Stef asked.

"I got it."

Stef was dying to know. But Jav closed the notebook and didn't offer. And Stef had to respect it.

But we wants it.

He rolled his eyes. *You can want without having, remember?*

Gollum snarled. *We wants to want and we wants to have.*

THEY ATE ON THE COUCH that night, watching *Planet Earth*. When he was done, Jav stacked a few pillows in his lap, using them as a desk to write more in his notebook.

"That was some big idea," Stef said.

"Yeah, it keeps leaving the room and coming back. 'Oh, and one other thing...'"

"Is this for your current book or the next one?"

Jav scratched over his ear with the end of the pen. "I don't know. It's just an idea."

He went back to writing. A bubble of swollen, jealous air between them on the couch that only Stef could see.

Oh knock it off, his inner shrink said. *You wouldn't want him breathing down the back of your neck while you were sketching or painting. What you really want to know is if he writes about you. That's what's going on here, right?*

He sighed softly. *Right.*

He goes to those deep, secret places in his mind and you're worried he forgets about you while he's there. Or rather, you wonder if he ever takes you with him.

"You ever illustrate a story?" Jav said.

Stef blinked. "No."

"Would you want to?"

"Yeah. Definitely. It would be cool. Why?"

"Just curious."

Stef reached toward the coffee table, tugging his sketchpad free from within a stack of magazines and books. He folded it back to the last page, where he'd drawn a variation of his Pegasi yin-yang symbol. Instead of winged horses, it was two men. One dressed in white, the other in black. Each nose to the other's knees. Wings sprouting from their shoulders and curving around to close the circle.

He handed the pad across the cushions. "I like illustrating our story."

Jav stuck the pen behind his ear and took the pad. He looked. He blinked. His lips parted as if to speak, then closed again as his finger reached to touch.

Stef sat still. Vulnerable and hopeful.

"This is us?" Jav said.

"Mm."

"When did you draw this?"

Stef shrugged. "Don't remember."

Now Jav looked at him. "Can I have it?"

Stef felt his face spread open. "Sure," he said, trying to sound casual. "Don't tear the page. I'll cut it out for you."

Jav put the sketchpad down. He took the pen from behind his ear and seemed poised to write again, then he closed his notebook and folded his hands over it. Seemingly done. He picked up the pad again, studied it, then set it aside.

Long minutes ticked by, narrated by David Attenborough's gravelly voice.

The stack of pillows fell over as Jav rose from the couch. Notebook tucked under his elbow, he picked up their plates. "Want another beer?"

"Nah, I'm good."

He was engrossed in the *Planet Earth* segment on cave diving when all of a sudden, something dropped between his gaze and the TV.

"Here," Jav said, holding his notebook open to a page. "It's not us, but it's... It's just an idea. But you can read it."

He walked away so fast, a breeze touched the back of Stef's neck. The bathroom door clicked shut.

Stef pointed the remote at the TV to lower the volume. His heart thumped as he read.

>*Trueblood goes to find the Pegasi.*
>
>*The winged horses don't interact with humans anymore. The sacred bond between man and horse has been broken. The Centaurs are no more and the Pegasi have no love for men.*

Trueblood needs a Pegasus in human form. He has to find the White Mare—only her foals can take human form.
(Why is that?
Maybe only the foals born of two mares can take human form?)

"The white mares," Stef mouthed, his eyes glancing up to the ceiling where, above him, his white-haired mother lived with her white-haired lover.

The Compass helps Trueblood find the Pegasi.
The White Mare's herd all have silver hooves. Her favorite foal is silver-grey with blue eyes. (Another sign he can take human form?)

What does Trueblood have to do to win the foal?
Fight?
Fight the foal or fight the White Mare?

Silver hooves.
Silver nose rings—are they born with these? The last vestige of when men and horses were bonded?
Maybe only foals born with the ring can take human form.
Trueblood has to fight to take ownership of a Pegasus. He has to take the ring to make the winged horse take human form.
It will be bonded to him. But not necessarily love him.

Trueblood fights the foal. It's long and brutal. Blood is drawn. The foal cracks the mariner's rib with a kick. Trueblood's sword slices above one of the foal's eyes. Blinded by blood, the winged horse falters and Trueblood takes the ring.
The White Mare's eyes are furious as she claps her wings together.
Thunder and lightning rip the skies open.
The foal transforms into a silver-haired man with blue eyes.
The silver hooves are now rings on his fingers.
His wings reduced to inked tattoos on his shoulder blades.

Stef's fingers extended on the page, the light catching on all his silver rings. The inked wings on his back tingled. His fingers wandered across the front of his shirt, along where the horse head was tattooed and circling the silver ring in his nipple.

A scar cuts through one of his eyebrows.
No love in his eyes for Trueblood.
Not yet.
The love will come later.
A love heavier than silver. Greater than thunder.
And it will come at a price.

A shiver crossed over Stef's skin. He closed the book and smoothed the cover. He hooked the loop of elastic around the pages to secure them shut. He held the notebook to his face a moment, inhaling the leather scent.

He got up and turned off the TV and the lights. Made sure the French doors and the front door were locked and the oven turned off.

He set the notebook on the desk.

He took one of his rings off and placed it on top.

"No price," he whispered.

ROOM SERVICE

"HEY," STEF SAID, letting his messenger bag slide to the floor as he heeled off his shoes.

"Still raining?" Jav said. He was standing in front of the open refrigerator door, staring down the shelves.

"Mm. What are you doing?"

"Trying to figure out something for dinner."

Stef's arms slid around Jav's waist and gave a curt tug.

"Hello," Jav sang as a rather enthusiastic hard-on clamored against his back pockets. "Is that your paycheck or are you just glad to see me?"

Stef slid a hand under Jav's T-shirt, gliding up his stomach and chest. "One guess."

Jav pushed back a little more. "You walk home with this?"

"I've been crossing my legs over it all goddamn day. Finally when I was coming down the stairs I let it fly." Now Stef's hand wormed down the front Jav's pants. "Don't mind me. What's for dinner?"

"Um..."

"Actually I'm not hungry."

"You don't say?"

Stef pushed the fridge door closed, turned Jav around and pressed him against it, kissing hard and deep. "You can be dinner."

"We never talk anymore."

"What do you want to talk about?"

Jav unbuckled Stef's belt. "We should discuss what you're going to do with this." He unbuttoned and unzipped the jeans and wrapped his hand around Stef's erection.

"Fuck," Stef groaned, his eyes closing and his head dropping back a little. He leaned harder on the palm against the fridge door. "Oh my God, man, I'm dying."

"Mm." Jav licked along the inked ocean wave on Stef's neck.

"Help me."

"What do you want?"

"Anything, I don't care."

"No, you want something. Tell me."

Stef turned his own mouth into Jav's neck, biting a little.

Jav slid and squeezed his hand. "Don't be shy, Finch."

"I want to be inside you."

"Thought so."

"I don't need t—"

"Can you wait ten minutes?"

Stef lifted up his head, flushed, his eyes glazed. "I can wait eleven. But you don't have t—"

Jav kissed him. "I want to."

"I fucking love you."

"I know."

He poured himself a shot of rum and downed it neat. "Report to the shower in ten minutes," he said, setting the glass down. "And you can bring me another one of these."

He didn't need to be blind drunk to bottom, but a bit of liquid courage helped him relax, as did a cascade of hot water down his back, steam in his lungs and the comforting proximity of soap. Even cleaned out, he felt less self-conscious about ass play in the shower.

He was cool with using the Fleets now. It was kind of crazy how fast they'd gone from an embarrassing big deal to a mindless, occasional part of nightly routine.

"Like nose hair trimming with benefits," Stef said.

Not to mention an empty Fleet box in the bathroom wastebasket made a silent but obvious signal someone was looking for some inside action. The adult version of a sock on the doorknob.

Jav surfed a little porn on his phone, waiting for the Fleet to do its thing. Truth be told, the prep was starting to be a bit of a turn-on. Now that he knew what was coming. Now that he knew the feel of Stef's fingers sliding deep inside him, curling around and into that *spot*. Jesus fucking Christ, when he'd knead at it while using his mouth or his hand at the same time. Jav shivered, now fully hard with the rum sinking golden fingers into his veins.

Once in the shower, he ran soaped-up fingers along his cock, edging himself and then backing down. Wondering if Stef was doing the same in the bedroom. No, he was in the bathroom now, his hand holding a shot glass easing around the curtain. "Room service."

Drinking in the shower was seriously underrated. "Gracias," Jav said, handing the glass back.

"De nada." Stef hit the dimmer switch, halving the light, knowing Jav was a little more comfortable when it was a little dark. He knew that like he knew not to talk too much, but follow Jav's verbal lead. If Jav cracked jokes, then Stef would too. If Jav were quiet and pulled inward, Stef stayed quiet, too. Their agreement was absolute in its wordlessness. Jav trusted Stef would be himself. Stef trusted Jav wouldn't try to be something he wasn't. If it didn't feel good, they stopped. No questions asked. No apologies necessary.

Tonight, despite all the build up, it didn't work out. Stef's fingers inside him felt great. He slid and turned them as they kissed with rum-sweet mouths. Slow and easy, getting Jav to open.

"Javi," he whispered around the water streaming down their faces. His lashes clumped into little spikes, his tattoos shining and sleek.

"God, you make me crazy," Jav said.

"You ready for me?"

Shaking and ready, Jav turned to the wall. But when Stef slid up behind him and slowly eased his cock inside, Jav knew right away he wasn't going to be able to take much. No matter how he shifted or angled, no matter if Stef moved slow or didn't move at all, Jav couldn't get on the other side of the burning ache.

Finally... "I gotta stop."

"All right. Hold still." Stef gently eased out and his arms wrapped around Jav's wet body. He held him tight as Jav took a few breaths and tried to get himself to unclench. He spit out water and the *sorry* loitering on his tongue. He didn't need it and Stef didn't want it.

"Open your hands," Stef murmured on his neck.

Jav smiled. He always forgot his hands. He pressed flat palms to the tile as Stef ran the spray cold and aimed it down the small of his back so it could numb the soreness. "Better?"

"Yeah."

"Let's get the fuck in bed."

They toweled dry, then lay down and picked up where they left off. It was so fucking easy. Mouths and hands and fingers and teeth and tongues. Knowing a hundred honest ways to make each other come into pieces was the only way to make love.

"I'm so in love with you," Jav whispered through his heaving chest.

Stef was breathing just as hard, mouth parted against the dim candlelight. "Say that again."

"I'm so in love with you."

"Tell me."

"Never felt this way about anyone." Jav swallowed. "Never felt this way about *me*."

THREE-INPUT

I was thrilled to hook Stavroula up with Roger Lark. It was my intention from the get-go. I mean *honestly*, are they made for each other or what? I don't feel a particularly strong pull to write their story right now but if I ever do, spoiler alert, Stav's getting knocked up with the sun-son and Roger will beg her, *beg* her not to leave him out of the decision. "I missed everything with Ari," he'll say. "I didn't even *know*."

Hard cut to Ari holding his new little brother, Sam Lark. Harder cut to Jav and Stef babysitting.

Sigh.

(By the way, none of that's written in stone.)

Anyway, Stav used to be a POV in the early drafts of *Finches*, until I narrowed it down to the triangle of three men. And this is just a little scribble about her meeting Roger for the first time. —SLQR

STAV GOES OUT TO DINNER with Rog, Stef and Jav.

"Best date ever," she says, looking around the handsome company. "Finally I can say every woman in the room wishes she were me."

"Everyone's wondering what the deal is," Stef says, opening a menu.

"Who's riding bitch on this cuddle train?" Rog says.

Jav raises his hand.

Stav bites back a three-input joke just as Stef kicks her under the

table. She bites the inside of her cheek harder.

After they order drinks, two women comes by the table, asking for Roger's autograph. He signs the bit of paper and makes polite, easy chit-chat, ending the exchange with a smooth but firm, "Enjoy your dinner."

"Does that happen often?" Stav asks when the fans are gone.

Roger shrugs. "Depends how unshaven I am." He looked at Jav. "You're next, pretty boy. Now that you're showing your face on book jackets, you'll be holding up traffic."

"He's already getting dick pics," Stef says.

"Some of them quite impressive," Jav says.

"Photoshop," Stav and Rog say at the same time. And smile at each other.

His face is so interesting. Such large features. Big nose, big smile, thick eyebrows. A quick side glance and he's awkward-looking and dorky. A second glance and he's quietly beautiful. Then he laughs and he's ridiculous.

He's a big man.

Next to him, Stav feels tiny.

She likes it.

She didn't feel small with her ex-husband. They knew each other since childhood. They grew up together at precisely the same pace and scale. They were exactly the same size. Twinned. She never had a sense he was physically protective of her.

Roger burns warm like a campfire next to her. His height and bulk, his tattoos and callused palms. He'd throw himself between her and danger. Stop a moving train. Lift up a car. Take a bullet.

All right, girlfriend, rein it in.

"She's in the zone," Jav says.

Stav blinks. "I'm sorry, what?"

Jav laughs. "You looked like I do when I get an idea out of nowhere."

Her face flames. "I was just...seeing something."

Roger's smile is kind but something in his face is wistful. Like he wants to see what she sees.

Stav looked around the table. "Remind me again, how do you know each other?"

The three men point and speak simultaneously.

"We're brothers," Roger says.

"He's Ari's father," Jav says.

"We're dating," Stef says.

"We are?" Roger says.

Exchanged glances through a beat of silence.

"Check, please," Stav says.

BARBED WIRE

A lot of readers ask me, "What about Ari and Deane?"

And I always think, *What about them?*

No disrespect to high school sweethearts that marry and stay together for the rest of their lives. I bow down to that shit, I think it's amazing. I also think it's rare. Ari and Deane love each other, but I never saw it as a forever love. Like so many other young teenage couples, they'd come to their natural end. Plus there's the whole cousin...thing.

A breakup however, makes for a wonderful opportunity for bonding with one's uncle. And, in Ari's case, for bonding with your uncle's partner.

By the way, if you are not familiar with the art of Pascal Campion, Google him and have it nearby during this chapter. Look at his use of light. How he captures little pure moments of human connection. That's Ari's technique. If my life story is ever made into a graphic novel, I want Pascal Campion to be the illustrator. —SLQR

ARI CAME TO MANHATTAN for Easter weekend. He stayed with Roger in the subletted apartment, but came down to Cushman Row for a visit. At his request, Jav made shrimp and yellow rice.

"So this is what a den of sin looks like," Ari said, then immediately put up a hand. "That came out wrong. Sorry. Never mind."

Jav was laughing. "It's okay. We're one of the tamer dens anyway."

As usual, he offered Ari a beer. As usual, Ari took it and wrinkled his nose above one or two sips. "Does nothing for me," he said. "I wish I could like it but I don't."

"It's an acquired taste."

"So I hear." Ari lifted the lid of the shallow pan with the rice and sniffed with appreciation. "Where's Stef?"

Jav jerked a thumb toward the bedroom. "Decompressing. Tough day at work."

"Isn't every day tough in that job?"

"Some are worse than others."

"Mm. How'd you guys meet?"

"It was when I went to Guelisten to return the keys to the apartment. He was looking at the gallery with Trelawney. I went upstairs and we just...met."

"Or maybe Trey orchestrated it?"

Jav laughed. "You know, it's entirely possible."

Ari grimaced over another pull of beer. "So you identify as gay now?"

"Bi."

"You still find women attractive?"

"Of course. So does Stef."

"But it's nothing you want to follow through with anymore."

"I don't know about things like anymore and nothing." Jav wiped off his hands. "I know that right now, I'm following this. Don't get me wrong, I have my share of *how the fuck did this happen* moments. But most of the time, it feels good and it feels like me."

"Gotcha." Ari gave him a sideways glance. "He seems like a good guy."

"He is."

"But if he fucks with your head, I'll kill him."

Jav raised his eyebrows. "Will you now?"

Ari shrugged. "I'd send a threatening text."

Underneath the sass, Ari seemed troubled. Like a ball of snarky barbed wire with a trembling egg at its center. Clearly something was up. And not for the first time, Jav felt his heart swell with love for this kid. Because maybe Ari came to New York to visit his biological father, but he came all the way downtown to seek solace from his uncle.

Because I had him first, Jav thought, then rolled his eyes. Dig him being all alpha male possessive. He bit his tongue and busied himself peeling shrimp and didn't push Ari to talk.

He heard Stef's voice: "Landes, what is this?"

Jav looked back over his shoulder. Stef stood by the counter, wet-haired and scowling, holding out a roll of bathroom tissue.

"That would be a roll of one-ply toilet paper, Finch."

"Oh, T, you didn't," Ari murmured.

Stef brandished the roll like it was a grenade. "What's the rule about one-ply toilet paper in this house?"

"Refresh my memory," Jav said.

Stef threw it at his head. "It does not *touch* my butt."

"Stef, I apologize," Ari said. "I'm embarrassed. I raised him better than this."

"He did," Jav said.

"One-ply," Stef said. "It's like I taught you nothing."

"It was on *sale.* I'm trying to budget here."

"We can cut the budget somewhere else. I don't want to see this prison crap in my bathroom again."

Ari pointed a stern finger at his uncle. "I am *very* disappointed in you."

"Okay, okay," Jav said. "Don't squeeze the Charmin."

Stef cracked a beer, drained a quarter of it, then turned a grin on Ari. "So what's *up*, man? What are you working on?"

Ari got his portfolio and showed some of the pieces from his digital art class.

"I'm into windows lately," he said. "Not sure why."

"Damn," Stef said, turning pages. "Jav, you seen these?"

"Not yet." Jav turned the burner down and went to look over their shoulders.

Page after page, Ari had captured intimate moments of human connection. Two people communing, with light being a third party. Sunshine slicing through a window into a darkened stairwell, where two lovers huddled on a tread. Interior light streaming out of buildings into the night, puddling around a couple walking a dog.

"The use of light is crazy," Stef said. "This is on the computer?"

"Yeah," Ari said. "Something about the medium just clicked with me. It's like all I want to do now. I haven't picked up a pencil in a week."

"This one," Jav said. "I want a print of this one." It was a bedroom at night. A girl sat on the windowsill, its frame wreathed in Christmas lights. Her hands wrapped around a mug. Snow fell outside. The twinkling garland splashed on the head of a boy sleeping in a twin bed. Or perhaps he was awake. And waiting.

"The composition is perfect," Stef said, framing the drawing with his thumbs and fingers. "Your eyes don't have to do any work. The emotion is quiet but it's just *tight.*"

"It's pure," Jav said.

"Yes." Stef pointed a finger. "Pure. Good word."

Soon Stef was taking out his own sketchbooks and pulling art books off the shelves, he and Ari jabbering over them while Jav cooked and watched. Both outside the moment and at the center of it.

Feels like home, he thought. *And it feels like me.*

All three men were quiet as they ate and watched TV. Ari kept glancing at Jav, then at Stef, his expression growing more worried. Stef threw a guarded, questioning look Jav's way but Jav could only shake his head.

"I don't know about you guys," Stef finally said. "But I'm jonesing for some ice cream." He got off the couch and slid his shoes on. "I'll just run out."

Jav counted twenty after he was gone. "Qué lo qué, Aaroncito?"

Ari just flipped a shoulder and stared straight ahead, his hand making long strokes along Roman's head.

"Think you want to talk about it?"

"I think growing up sucks."

"That it does."

Ari changed the channel, ostensibly putting an end to the conversation. Jav let it go. Stef came back with four pints of Ben & Jerrys. They heaped bowls high and watched the Knicks get crushed until it wasn't fun anymore. Ari clicked off the TV then, and silence descended with all the subtlety of the ceiling collapsing.

"You going to stay tonight?" Stef asked, scraping his bowl. "Or head back uptown."

"I don't know," Ari said. "Deane and I might break up."

Mouth closed around his spoon, Stef's eyes met Jav's then flicked away.

"Oh," Jav said.

"She's..." Ari pushed the heel of his hand into his eyes. "*Fuck*."

Jav put his bowl down. "It's all right."

"I don't know what to do. Everything's changing."

"I know."

And you're young, Jav thought. *You're in college. You're hot-blooded and meeting new people. The world's getting bigger. Your perception is widening. Your heart's starting to get crowded.*

"I spent a lot of time with Roger this winter," Ari said. He glanced at Stef. "Roger's my dad. My real dad, I mean."

"I know," Stef said quietly.

"We went skiing over President's Day weekend. Just us two. He comes to see me at school. A lot of times, we go over to Guelisten. Have dinner with Alex and Val. And Trelawney. So it's... I don't know."

"You're spending time with your family," Stef said.

"Yeah."

"Not your girlfriend's family who's being kind and hospitable to you because you go to school nearby. This is your father and his sisters. Your blood relatives."

Ari bit his lips hard, his face twisting. "I'm so fucking confused now."

"I can tell, man. I'm sorry." Stef gathered up all the bowls and took them back to the kitchen. Roman followed, collar tags jingling and for a single, tight, beautiful instant, they were all of them a family.

It's so pure, Jav thought, bewildered. *How did this happen?*

"It was really simple for a while," Ari said. "I didn't *care*. I swear it made no difference to me. She was all I wanted. The one...thing. The one. And it was all bright and beautiful and perfect. But now..."

"It's not so simple," Stef said, coming back to the couch.

"Every since I started spending time with Rog and getting to know him, I've been so much more aware. Val texts me to say hi or Trelawney checks in or Alex... I'm just so aware of it now, T. Deane's my cousin.

Her mother is my father's sister and..."

"It bothers you," Jav said.

"I don't know if *bother* is the right word, but I'm thinking about it. More and more."

"What about Deane?"

"We've been talking about it. More and more."

"I see."

"God, you know, all my life, family came in and out of my life. I went from feeling I had no one to feeling I had just one someone. You. Then I found out I have a lot of someones. I'm looking at pictures on Val's wall and thinking, *Jesus, these are my grandparents.*"

Jav nodded. "They're Deane's grandparents, too."

"Crap, it wasn't weird when it still had some distance. But now it's kind of sinking in and it's just a little weird."

"Yeah."

"God, she's so smart."

"Who?" Stef said.

"Val. She's the one who said, 'Love each other and see what happens.'"

Jav laced his hands behind his head. "She's a smart lady, Valerie Lark."

"I can't lie, T. I was thrilled to pieces finding out she was my aunt. Trelawney's one of the coolest people on the planet, and to find out she's my aunt too? I'm related to Aunt Cool? That makes me cool by blood. I have cool DNA on both sides now."

Jav looked at Stef. "Did he just compliment me?"

"Sounded like it," Stef said.

"I have to do it sneakily." Ari scrubbed at his face. "I'm lucky," he said between his fingers. "I feel confused as hell right now but I'm trying to see past that and remember I got really fucking lucky with everything." His phone pinged and he wrestled it out of his pocket. "See?" he said, turning it toward Jav. "My old man is asking if I'm okay."

"Are you okay?"

Texting, Ari's foot jostled Jav's on the coffee table. "I got you, don't I?"

He opted to go back uptown for the night. Stef went up to hail a cab while Jav packed up shrimp and rice to have for tomorrow.

"Hasta mañana," Ari said, hugging Jav on the outside steps. He turned and hugged Stef then. "Thanks, man."

"It'll all work out," Stef said. "You're right where you're supposed to be."

The two men hung on the steps, watching the cab drive off. When it was out of sight, Stef's hand slid up the back of Jav's neck.

"Landes, did I just become an aunt?"

Jav turned wide eyes on him. "Finch, I don't know *what* the fuck just happened."

JAV HAD A MEETING with his editor the next day. It went long, and when he got back to Cushman Row, Ari was there, sitting at the kitchen counter with his sketchpad.

Looking over the boy's shoulder, Jav saw Ari was drawing Stef, who was asleep on the couch. One arm over his head and one bare foot sticking out of the throw blanket. His other arm curled around Roman, who had inserted himself between Stef's body and the cushions. The slice of gold light from the standing lamp lit up the one foreleg resting on Stef's chest.

"Nice," Jav said.

"The perspective is fucked up," Ari said, his eyes glancing up, then down.

"Cool how you can't really see Roman. Just his paw."

"Mm." Eyes up, eyes down. Pencil moving in long strokes, then in fine little stabs. Coaxing Stef off the paper without disturbing his sleep.

Jav's heart curled into a fist, then released, flooding his veins with love and gratitude. He leaned and kissed Ari's head. "Verdad de mi sangre."

Ari's eyes didn't leave his subject, his hand didn't stop moving. "Te quiero, Tío," he murmured over his work.

You've Been Here Before

This seems a good time to pause and talk about Jav and Ari for a couple of chapters. And Geno as well. For those of you who like the behind-the-scenes tour of how my characters are crafted, you'll like this. If not, go on and skip ahead. No hard feelings.

"If my parents had changed one letter of my name, I could've had a whole different life," Jav said. "This is the kind of shit I think about."

Jav actually did start out as Xavier. Xav for short. But I'm never confident pronouncing Xavier and it's a French name, besides. I was reluctant to write another sexy Francophone. Who could surpass Will?

So he became Javier. The name change was just one of dozens of incarnations Jav took on. He wasn't an escort from the get-go. He started out as a junior parole officer. Then he was a public defender. Then a social worker. He was gay at first. Then I made him straight. But no, I think maybe he was bi. No, gay. No, wait...

Ari's name was always Aaron Seaver but in the beginning, he was no relation to Jav. In my early scribblings for *Larks*, there's a 9-1-1 transcript and a newspaper article to introduce Ari and his circumstances. I'll show them to you now. —SLQR

DISPATCH: MORGANTOWN 9-1-1 [Inaudible] Where is the exact location of your emergency?

Caller: 15 Brookside Drive I need the police here

Dispatch: 16 Brookside and you need police

Caller: 15 Brookside. One-five. My mom is [inaudible]

Dispatch: Sir? What is your name, sir?

Caller: Ari Seaver. I need help.

Dispatch: Tell me what's happening.

Seaver: Mom's boyfriend is beating her up, you need to send someone. 15 Brookside, you've been here before.

Dispatch: I have a patrol car seven blocks from your street, they're on the way. Where is your mother now?

Seaver: He's gonna kill her

Dispatch: Ari, where is your mother now?

Seaver: In the bedroom. With him. He's got them locked in with the dog. The dog's going crazy. I can't get in. [Background noise] Mom.

Dispatch: Ari, get away from the door.

Seaver: Leave her alone [expletive]. Jesus Christ, the dog.

Dispatch: Are there weapons in—

Seaver: Mom

Dispatch: Ari listen to me, are there weapons in the house?

Seaver: He's got guns, yeah, I know he does.

Dispatch: Where are they?

Seaver: I have no [expletive] idea. [Background noise]. Oh Jesus Christ. [Inaudible].

Dispatch: Ari, tell me what's happening.

Seaver: Oh Christ.

Dispatch: Have the police arrived?

Seaver: No. I don't know. The dog isn't barking anymore. [Background noise]. Mom [expletive]. [Background noise]. I gotta go in.

Dispatch: Ari no. Get away from the door. Wait for the police.

Seaver: I'm going in. He's gonna kill her. Mom. [Expletive].

Dispatch: Ari.

[Background noise]

Dispatch: Ari. Get away from the door.

[Background noise]

Dispatch: Ari.

[Background noise]

Dispatch: Ari.

[Call terminated]

MORGANTOWN, NY (WPXL)

A 16-year-old Morgantown boy is being held without bail until a Thursday court hearing after investigators say he beat a man with a baseball bat. Neighbors say the boy acted in self-defense when he allegedly assaulted his mother's boyfriend.

Police responded to a domestic-related assault call Friday night, just before 10 pm, on Brookside Drive. When officers arrived, they found the owner Maggie Seaver unconscious and Craig Frante suffering from blunt-force trauma to the head.

Detectives interviewed the 16-year-old, Ari Seaver, Saturday morning. Neighbors told WPXL that Frante lived at the house and had been reportedly involved with Mrs. Seaver for the past two years. The relationship was abusive, they told WPXL:

"We've seen police at that house a half-dozen times," a neighbor who didn't want to be identified said. "A bad situation that just got worse."

Multiple neighbors told WPXL they heard noise and commotion coming from 15 Brookside on the night in question. Matthew Fragiacomo, who was taking out his garbage, said he approached the house but then backed off to call police. Two additional 911 calls report a domestic disturbance on Brookside at the same time Ari Seaver made his own emergency call.

Frante allegedly locked himself and Mrs. Seaver in an upstairs bedroom, along with the family dog. Mr. Seaver allegedly broke the doorknob off with a baseball bat and gained entry, then assaulted Frante with the bat.

Detectives found both Frante and Mrs. Seaver in the upstairs bedroom. Medics pronounced Mrs. Seaver dead on scene. The family dog was also found to be dead. Frante was transported to Ash Memorial Hospital where he is listed in critical condition.

Mr. Seaver was arrested and charged with assault with a deadly weapon which was changed to aggravated assault by the District Attorney's Office.

"This isn't a violent kid," said Christopher Jensen, a teacher at Morgantown High school. "He's a quiet guy, a good student, doesn't

make trouble. From what I understand, he was just protecting his mother."

Ari Seaver is being held in the juvenile section of an adult correctional facility. At Thursday's status hearing, a judge will meet with the case's prosecutor and defense attorney, a district attorney's office representative said. A number of decisions can happen from the status hearing, including the decision of whether to take the case to trial.

Edited to add: The Seaver's dog was not killed in the incident as originally reported, rather the animal was reportedly taken to Morgantown Animal Hospital for treatment. Dr. Andrew Penda**, DVM, told WPXL the dog is in critical, but stable condition.

[**Alex used to be Andrew. Deane was Alex but then I gave Alex to her father and she was called Andie for a while, short for Anne Deane. Then she became Deane. Rhymes with mean. —SLQR]

THE ADVOCATE'S CAPE

My early idea for Ari was he'd be charged with aggravated assault and sentenced to two years probation at Lark House. His probation officer was Javier Landes, son of the Morgantown Police Chief. No wait, he's a public defender. No, a social worker. Oh hell, whatever he is, his mentor-like relationship with Ari brings him into contact with Dr. Penda and the Lark family and all the drama therein.

You have to do a lot of playing around to give complex characters a simple story. But here, I'll show you. What follows is transcribed straight out of one of the *Larks* notebooks. —SLQR

STILL PLAYING AROUND with Ari's circumstances.

I could have his biological father be dead and his single mother be a drug addict or killed by an abusive boyfriend, but it kind of mirrors Erik's missing father situation. Been there, done that.

Besides, you really want him to have killed someone? Would he be able to psychologically handle that? You want him in court? On probation? Can you make this simpler? Get rid of any criminal acts, pre-meditated or otherwise?

I could have his mother be dead and his father the drug addict Possibly have his father be gay and subsequently murdered by a lover/dealer. Or he could just OD. He OD's one night and then the dog ends up eating the rest of the heroin...

Let's say the mother is gone and the father is an addict/dealer. Ari has managed to survive this situation by becoming as invisible as possible. School and a part time job. He has to hide his money and possessions because his father will just sell anything and everything for his habit. He's cleaned out Ari's college savings fund. Ari's dismissed his chances for art school and now his goal is to get an apprenticeship with a tattoo artist and maybe day one day open his own shop. Or at least work at one. Make enough money to get out of here and survive. In the meantime, lay low, stay invisible, hide your valuables. With the money he makes from working, he buys food for Roman and pays his cell phone bill. Roman is his life, his phone is his lifeline.

But he sees horrible shit. Experiences unspeakable things.

One night he comes home. The house is unlocked and quiet. Roman doesn't come to greet him. His father is dead or close to death. The dog is unconscious.

Ari calls 911. Police and paramedics arrive, including Sargent Rafael Landes. He's the one who calls Animal Control and they get the dog transferred to the Hudson Bluffs Humane Society where Andy Penda is the on-call emergency vet (this comes out later).

So here's this seventeen-year-old boy, distraught, upset, possibly in shock. A crowd of neighborhood gawkers has gathered during the scene but now they all seem to melt away into the shadows, distancing themselves. The Seavers' house has long been suspected as a crack den. Rumors abound of tricks being turned and so forth. They don't want to be associated. Some of them may have dealings with Phil Seaver they'd rather keep off the record. It's not a good neighborhood in Morgantown and Sargent Landes knows it.

Sargent Landes is also a big dog lover. And his son, Javier, is a county social worker.

"Why don't you come back to the precinct with me? Get you warmed up with a cup of coffee and we'll figure some things out. Talk about what's going to happen next."

Ari hesitates.

"You were at work tonight?" Landes asks.

"Yeah."

"Someone can verify that?"

"Eight people can verify that."

"Then you're not in trouble. You're not under arrest. Let's get you away from this scene, all right?"

Ari has some questions. His most valuable things are in his room—cash, art supplies, sketchbooks. Maybe Sgt. Landes calls over a detective who can make some assurances. The house will be sealed as a crime scene but it seems an open-and-closed case. Ari will be able to return and collect his possessions.

Ari goes with Landes back to the precinct. Refuses the coffee. Takes a bottle of water but doesn't drink it. An officer brings him a doughnut.

Sgt. Landes calls his son. It's late but Jav comes. He's greeted heartily by the force. They've known him since he was a child.

Jav's mother has refused to see or speak to him since Jav came out. Rafael was upset by the news and while he's never met any of Jav's partners, he remains close with his son and they spend a lot of time together.

Jav's a county social worker but also volunteers with the Hudson Bluffs Mentor Project. He's been a tireless child advocate but six months ago, one of his mentees committed suicide. Jav took it hard. This, coupled with his ongoing estrangement with his mother, is putting Jav under a lot of stress, and putting a strain on the current relationship with his partner, Thomas.

[Yes, *that* Thomas. He started out as Jav's partner and ended up Stef's fuck buddy. Weird how these things evolve. —SLQR]

He doesn't arrive at the precinct with any of his past piss-and-vinegar. No advocate's Superman cape. He figures he'll get the kid transferred over to the Halfway House associated with Morgantown Correctional Facility and they'll take it from there. He'll push some papers, give a ride and go back home to bed.

Jav comes into the room where Ari is. Ari's been drawing on some scrap paper. One look and Jav's abuse bells go off. Though cloaked in a heavy leather jacket, he can see this boy is just short of emaciated. This isn't natural thinness but something that reeks of starvation. He feels the advocate's cape start to creep up his back. Something isn't right here.

He introduces himself, asks permission to close the door and if he can sit down.

"I'm really sorry about what happened tonight," he says.

Ari nods, looking a little confused. As if nobody has yet expressed their sympathy to him tonight and like he wouldn't know what to do with it anyway.

"The police are saying you have no other family?"

Ari shakes his head.

"No friends? No place you can go tonight?"

Again the head shakes and the eyes defy further questioning.

"A teacher you trust at school? A coach? Someone from church?"

A snort of laughter with the head shake this time but the boy's eyes grow a little more liquid.

Jav runs his hands through his hair. "Ari... I'm sorry, man. I feel like shit about this. And I want to take you somewhere safe tonight."

"Can I see my dog?" The voice is surprisingly deep and strong, coming from this slender boy.

"I can't do that tonight but if you let me take you somewhere safe, I promise I'll make some calls and get you to your dog as soon as I can."

Looking away, Ari nods.

"You'll let me?"

He keeps nodding. A long pause unfolds.

"Are you hungry?" Jav asks.

"No."

Jav looks at the unopened bottle of water and the untouched doughnut. "When was the last time you ate something?"

A shrug of leathered shoulders. A jingle of zippers as they fall.

Jav's eyes narrow. There was heroin in the house. The boy doesn't look high. Nor does he look in withdrawal. Jav weighs the future against the bit of trust he's established tonight. The first girders of a bridge. If he's going to blow it up, best he do it now and not later on when there's more to lose.

"I'm going to ask you to do something for me, Ari."

Ari looks at him, every sharp line in his gaunt face etched with exhaustion. The eyes are barely holding on.

"Will you show me your arms?"

A beat. Then the eyes flare into life. "What, you think I'm fucking high?"

Jav holds his gaze and holds still.

In a jarring, explosive movement, Ari rips off his jacket. He wears a short-sleeved T-shirt beneath, his arms like pipestems in the sleeves. He thrusts them over the desk toward Jav. Blue veins at his wrists and at the juncture of his elbows in clear, pale skin. No track marks. "Happy?"

"Very," Jav says quietly.

"I don't touch that shit."

"Thank you for showing me."

The hands curl into fists. "You have no fucking idea what it was like."

"No, I don't."

Ari stands up abruptly, his chair falling over backwards behind him. With something close to a sneer, he goes for his belt buckle. "Want me to drop 'em? You want to check my legs next, right? When my old man couldn't find veins in his arms anymore, he went for his feet. But your feet suck for shooting up. Veins are too small, it's hard to register a hit. And it takes forever to reach your brain..."

Tired himself and weary of the world where things like this are allowed to happen, Jav stares back stupidly.

"There's a great vein in your groin," Ari says. "But he was scared to use that one. A friend of his missed the vein and got the artery once. Man, that was some fucked up shit."

"Ari—"

"You want to know the last time I ate? At home? My old man had better things to do with money. And with me."

Jav stands up slowly, walks around the desk to right Ari's chair. "Tell me." He sits again but Ari doesn't.

"When he had no money left? Oh, then it got fun. Shit started disappearing right and left. Electronics first. Then appliances. My mother's jewelry. My art supplies, until I started locking them up. Motherfucker cleaned out my college savings. I had to start hiding my cash. He'd beat the shit out of me looking for it. And then he—"

He cuts off so fast, another alarm goes off in Jav's head. A surge of anger behind his eyeballs.

Not good. This is not good.

"He what?" Jav says softly.

"Nothing." Ari sits, breathing hard. "I got nothing now. Nothing except my dog. He's all I got."

"I'll get you to him. I promise."

A long time while Ari pulls himself together. Jav wishes he would cry and prays he doesn't.

Slowly, Ari pulls his jacket back on. "So where's this haven you're taking me?"

With little thought, Jav's original plan of the county's halfway house is scrapped. "Lark House," he says. "In Guelisten."

A grunted chuckle. "Where the rich people live? What's a juvy home doing there?"

"It's not juvy. It's a group home for transitional living."

"The fuck does that mean?"

"Kids who are too old to be placed in foster care. Or kids who have aged out of foster care and are transitioning into independent living. It's also a shelter for runaway teens."

Ari picks up the pencil and twirls it through his fingers. "When do you age out?"

"Eighteen."

"I'm seventeen."

Going on forty, Jav thinks. "I know."

"So... What, I belong to the state now?"

"Unless your parents named a legal guardian in their will. Did they have a will?"

"Doubt it."

"Did they have a safe deposit box? Strongbox?"

"They sold everything."

"You can't sell papers. We'll get into the house to look."

"But if there's nobody, and there isn't, I'm a ward of the state until I'm eighteen?"

Jav nods this time.

"So who's gonna..." Ari looks around, mouth working to formulate a question. "Who's gonna help me?"

"I am."

A long moment of eye contact, through which Ari blinks.

"This place... Lark House?"

"It's a good place," Jav says. "One of the best. Privately run."

"It's not like a...you know."

"Jail?"

"Yeah."

"No. It's not Morgantown. It's not a detention center."

"I don't want anyone..." Ari swallows and looks away. "I don't want anyone touching me."

Oh dear God. "No one will touch you." Jav's throat aches over the words and he digs fingernails hard into his leg to keep it together.

"I mean it. I'll sleep on the street first."

"No one will touch you. Go there tonight. We'll only look at tonight. You can get something to eat. A hot drink. A place to put your head down. It's safe. I give you my word."

"Do I have to go?"

Jav thinks about it. "If they release you to me, then technically I have to take you somewhere secure. I'm accountable." He attempts humor. "I could ask my father if there's room here in the holding tank?"

"Who's your father?"

"Sargent Landes. White hair. Gold tooth here." Jav points to one of his own incisors. Rafael lost that tooth in a drug bust ten years ago. The gold replacement was his reward to himself.

"He's the one who called Animal Control," Ari says absently. The pencil is properly in his fingers now and he's sketching a series of lines.

"He loves dogs."

"You have one?"

I have Thomas, Jav thinks. "No. My apartment building doesn't allow pets."

Ari sighs, pushes the paper away. "All right."

"All right?"

"I'll go. I'm tired."

"You've been tired a long time."

Ari nods.

Jav drives Ari to Lark House. They're kind there. He's shown to a room and Ari seems glad its door can be locked from the inside. They get him a toothbrush, a pair of sweatpants. A charger for his phone.

"Are you hungry?"

Ari seems fascinated with the new toothbrush in its shrink wrapping. "No."

Jav leaves his business card. "I'll come back in the morning." Which is only a few hours away. He's supposed to meet Thomas for breakfast but fuck it, Thomas is getting on his last nerve these days anyway. To the point where Jav will spend a night on his parents' couch and deal with his mother ignoring him.

HIS FATHER'S ARM

You can start to see it, right? Or at least, you can start to see Jav and Ari. They're just cloaked in different costumes.

I let them keep trying things on. They led and I followed. Anything that came into my weird head went down on paper, no questions asked.

Sometimes, though, a thing goes from my head to the paper to the final draft almost perfectly intact. While everything around it shifts and rearranges and tangles, the idea stays magically the same and I know it belongs.

After sketching the scenes you just read, I wrote four chapters which made it almost verbatim into the final draft of Larks. When Jav picks Ari up from Lark House and they go to the coffee shop. Deane comes running through, steals a danish and Ari's heart as well. Ari reuniting with his dog, meeting Alex. Going to the diner with Jav and then back to Lark House, exhausted and overwhelmed. These things were gelang from the start.

Sometimes things don't belong. Not that they aren't good. It's just not their time. I started down a road with Ari and couldn't continue, because his story would've become the whole book. It wasn't something I could touch on a little and then have easily or magically resolved.

Simply put, what ended up being Geno Caan's story was originally Ari's story.

I'll show you. —SLQR

THE CLOTHES ARI COLLECTED from home are dirty so a staff member shows him where the laundry room is. In the dining hall he eats some mashed potatoes. There's a library and he finds a couple books which he takes back to his room. He collects his clothes from the dryer, hugs the big warm armful and inhales.

Back in his room he gets out one of his sketchbooks and his pencils. His favorite way to draw is kneeling at the side of the bed and working on the mattress. He falls into his work, drawing bits of Deane Penda. A single grey eye, golden flecks by the pupil. He turns the page and sketches her leg. His thumb shades, bringing out the muscle definition.

He puts the pencil down, turns away from the bed and pitches forward onto his hands. He tries, for the first time in years, to do some pushups. He used to be able to fall out bed in the mornings and crank out a hundred. He can barely do ten now. His arms tremble and his heart bangs wildly against his ribs.

He's so tired.

Heart still thumping, he breaks the new toothbrush out of its plastic wrap and uses it.

He gets into bed. Behind his closed lids he sees warm honey hair and grey eyes. Sculpted legs. For the first time in years, his own hand slides down the front of his sweatpants.

He falls asleep smiling.

He wakes out of a dream, his stomach iron, the bile rising up in the back of his throat. Moonlight coming through the window reflects off the crumpled plastic wrap on the desk.

"You play sports?" Deane Penda had asked.

"Not anymore."

Once, Ari played football and wrestled. He was all-county his freshman year. Sophomore year, his coaches talked of scholarships. He was sixteen. Fit and built and strong. He had a girlfriend with a heart-shaped ass who loved to fuck him. Female eyes followed wherever he went.

Then his father's eyes started growing desperate. Things

124

disappeared. The house grew bare. Ari went to take money out from the ATM and *overdrawn* flashed up on the screen.

His father had friends over. Dealers. His father would sell anything to get a fix.

Eyes followed him. Watching as he ate. He was an athlete. He ate constantly. He had a lot of muscle to feed.

It must have been in his food that first time. Rohypnol or liquid ecstasy or Special K. It wasn't enough to knock him out. Too much muscle. But enough to keep him from fighting back when that hand went down the front of his sweatpants.

His father made two hundred bucks.

"Two fifty if they didn't have to slip you something," his father said afterward. "You got what these guys want. They have what I want. You could help me out and take a cut. Start pulling your weight around here."

Ari learned quickly not to eat at home. Like a suspicious medieval king, he ate nothing he hadn't kept his eyes on at all stages of preparation. Nothing he didn't see others eat first.

Then they got him by putting the shit on his toothbrush.

Another two hundred in his father's arm.

He started brushing his teeth at school. He stopped eating. The muscle melted away as he tried to rid himself of what those guys wanted. To have the least amount of weight to pull. He dropped football first. Then wrestling. Then the girlfriend. He got two after school jobs so he could buy his own security detail. One salary he turned over to his father. The other he lived on, including buying Roman's food.

The last time, about a month ago, he wasn't drugged. He guarded his mouth but forgot to check his back. Two guys held him down for the third who had two hundred bucks to spend. He had grey eyes. He kissed Ari before going on his shopping spree.

From Ari's mouth to his father's arm. All the while Roman barked and howled from the back yard, clawing at the kitchen door.

Lark House is sleeping. Ari creeps down the hall to the communal bathroom and throws up until he has nothing anybody wants and no weight to pull. Back in bed, he keeps his mouth shut against the fiery sobs trying to break free. Nothing goes in. Nothing comes out.

So you can see how I start out with grandiose plots that get chiseled down to simpler stories, and while Ari was still beset by tragedy beyond his control, this particular tragedy of rape and forced prostitution would not end up being his. Still, writing it served a few purposes. It planted the idea that a male victim of rape would make an interesting story. It also gave me the idea that maybe Jav gets so emotionally invested in this kid's story because once upon a time, it was Jav selling himself to survive.

Which turned out to be a thing. —SLQR

EXACTLY WHAT I WANTED

This is some early, slightly chemical interaction between Jav and Alex. Remember at this stage of the game, Jav wasn't an escort, he and Alex had never met before and he identified as gay. —SLQR

A FEW WEEKS AFTER MEETING, Alex calls Jav one night. Guelisten Animal Shelter is expecting an emergency drop-off, a rescue operation of seventeen dogs from an abusive situation. They need to clear as much space as possible. Alex will take Roman to his house and keep him there.

"But I don't want Ari to... I just want him to be aware and give his consent," Alex says. "You know, like he has control over the situation?"

Silence on the other end.

Alex feels dumb and intrusive and he's not sure why. "If we could draw something up? An agreement that I'm just holding him temporarily? You know, make it official?"

It's awkward. Jav is answering in rather terse monosyllables.

Finally, "Listen, am I calling at a bad time?" Alex says.

A pause. "I'm on a date."

"Oh. Shit, I'm sorry. I'll—"

"No, don't worry. I understand what you're getting at and it's a good idea. I'll let him know and we'll figure something out."

"No worries. Whenever. Sorry to interrupt."

"It's fine. I'll call you tomorrow, okay?"

"Sure."

Next day, Jav is stiff and reticent when he brings Ari over to see Roman. Val seduces Ari with food. He and Deane bond over music and artwork and dogs.

"Let him stay a while," Alex says. "You can pick him up later or I'll drive him back to Lark House."

He walks Jav to his car. A bit of small talk through the driver's side window.

"I'm sorry about last night," Alex says.

"There's nothing to be sorry for, knock it off."

"Is something wrong?"

Jav stares straight ahead a moment, knuckles tight on the steering wheel. He drops his forehead, laughs a little. "It was a shitty date."

"Oh."

"I was desperately looking for an excuse to get the hell out of there. And then my phone rang and it was you. It threw me off." Reaches for seatbelt and buckles it.

"Threw you off?"

"Never mind."

"No, what?"

"It's just that... It was exactly what I wanted. On a lot of levels."

"What do you mean?"

Jav smiles, shaking his head. "Nothing. Give me a ring or text me, let me know about Ari. He has to be back at Lark House by ten."

"No problem." Alex's gaze gets snagged on Jav's. A tiny electric frisson passes between them. Almost like chemistry.

Chemistry? What the fuck?

Foreign and disturbing as the idea is, he still feels reluctant to let Jav drive away.

"What was wrong with her?" he asks.

"Her who?"

"Your date."

Jav puts the car in gear. "Him."

Alex blinks. "Oh."

Jav drives away.

J AV GOES OVER TO T ULIP S TREET one day. Alex is sitting at the bottom of the staircase, his back against the wall, feet against the newel post. Halfway up the stairs, the Lark-Penda's kitten, Esmeralda, is perched on a tread, mewing pathetically. On each step leading down to Alex is a little bit of cat kibble.

"What are you doing?" Jav says, leaning on the banister.

"Teaching her to come down." Alex looks up and makes a whispering noise between his teeth. Esmeralda whines. She puts down a trembling front paw to the next tread and takes it back. She turns around and tries lowering a back paw but that doesn't work. She cries.

"Dude, you're so mean," Jav says.

"She can do it," Alex says. The light comes in the stairwell window and shines grey-green in his eyes. His lips move around that whispered beckon. "Come here," he says. "Come."

Jav swallows, briefly closing his eyes and wondering what that whisper sounds like against skin. In the dark.

"That's it," Alex says as Esmeralda takes another step and eats her reward. "See?"

She mews at him. He mews back, then laughs. "Drama queen."

Jav watches, fascinated and longing as step by step, the kitten makes her way down to Alex. He picks her up in one big hand and rubs her face against his. "Good girl," he says, laughing. "Look at that, huh? You did it."

He curls her in a palm, feeds her another treat and tucks her against his chest. Above her head he grins at Jav. Tousled and unshaven. Body relaxed and muscular in jeans and a flannel shirt. "Tough love, man. It's how they learn."

Come, Jav thinks. *Come here. You can do it…*

HARRIS TWEED

I wanted so much for Ari and Geno to become friends. They'd complement each other beautifully and I can totally see Geno continuing his education at New Paltz. But there's only so much you can pack into an epic novel. —SLQR

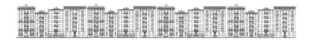

JAV INVITED GENO to come see his nephew's art exhibit at SUNY New Paltz.

"Is this crossing the smudged boundary?" Geno said to Stef.

"Only if you punch me."

"Awkward."

"Sorry."

He, Jav and Stef took the subway uptown to meet up with Roger Lark, The Treehouse Guy.

"My mother had a *thing* for you," Geno said as they shook hands.

"I get that a lot," Roger said. "And may I say, nice jacket?"

Geno was wearing Nathan's Harris tweed jacket, nearly identical to the one Roger was sporting.

"It was my father's," Geno said.

"So was mine," Roger said. "Apparently fathers are required to own one and pass it down to their sons."

"Well, I feel cheated," Jav said, shrugging into his own jacket, a handsome brown corduroy one.

Geno dozed off for the first part of the drive, lightly suspended in the hum of three deep, male voices over music. When he woke up they'd crossed the river and were heading up the Thruway.

He'd never been to this part of New York. The Hudson Valley was pretty under a peach-pink sunset, and New Paltz was a funky little town. The campus was sprawling and handsome, a man-made lake thinning into a winding creek all through the residential area.

"It's like Venice or something," Geno said.

"One day when you see Venice, you'll laugh at this moment," Roger said, grinning.

A strange and unexpected shyness came over Geno as he was introduced to Ari Seaver. He couldn't quite pinpoint why, only that it felt like he hadn't met anyone his age in months. Ari had Roger's strong nose and jaw, and Jav's dark hair and slanting eyebrows.

Geno wandered through the gallery, ending at Ari's section. He stopped dead, staring at a small, five-by-five canvas. Painted on it was a little red house in the twilight gloaming, golden light streaming out of its windows.

The voices in the gallery receded into a faint hum. Geno stood motionless, lips parted, falling into the picture.

There it is, he thought. *Just the way I've always pictured it.*

"Hey." Ari appeared at Geno's side.

"Hey." He pointed. "This is... This is kind of my life right here."

"Yeah?" Ari's eyes, so like Jav's, were full of interest and patience.

"Yeah. See." He cleared his throat. "My mother died when I was fifteen."

"Mine too. I was seventeen."

Gene blinked. "Was she sick?"

Ari shook his head. "Fell down the stairs and broke her neck."

"Jesus."

"Yeah." Ari's quick smile and shrug was like a club's secret handshake. "But you were saying?"

"So her maiden name was Gallinero. It's Spanish for henhouse and— Do you speak Spanish?"

"Not well enough to have this conversation. Go on."

Now Geno's shoulders twitched, trying to push off this weird bashfulness and tell a simple story. Ari listened quietly, his eyes flicking from Geno to the painting and back again.

"Anyway," Geno said. "It looked like that. Exactly like that. The way the light spills out of the windows, it's like I was dictating it. I mean, like you reached in my head and put it down on the canvas."

"Wow. That's crazy."

"Holy shit," Stef said over their shoulders. "Am I seeing what I think I'm seeing?"

"Right?" Geno said. "I'm kind of losing my mind here."

"You're not the only one." Stef nudged Ari and pointed. "Cleanup on aisle eleven."

At another wall, Jav was having his own staring moment. Tearing himself away from the little red house, Geno went over to look.

This canvas was larger. A ship's darkened cabin. Boots dropped on the wooden floor. A sword belt hanging from a chair. Two tankards and a wine bottle on a little table. In Ari's signature style, milky moonlight streamed through a single porthole to splash onto a narrow bed. A man slept there. Bare-chested with an arm thrown over his head and a foot sticking out of the bedclothes. Another man slept beside him, obscured in darkness except for one muscular arm slung across the first man's chest. The moonlight showed a ship's wheel tattooed on his forearm. A wheel Geno immediately recognized from Jav's arm.

He squinted at the painting's caption: *Verdad de mi sangre.*

"Truth of my blood?" he said.

"Trueblood," Ari said, sliding an arm around his uncle. "You like it?"

"I hate it," Jav said, his voice gruff.

"It's yours. Your birthday present. I'll bring it home to you after the show closes."

Jav ran the back of his hand across his eyes. "You're killing me."

Geno backed quietly away from the intimate moment and returned to his commune with the little red house.

Roger was staying the night in New Paltz, so Geno rode alone with Jav and Stef in the SUV. Once again dozing in the backseat. Feeling safe with his big brothers navigating. Peeking occasionally through his eyelashes to watch Stef's hand cross the console and rub the back of Jav's neck. Jav reached back to take it and drove for a while with Stef's fingers against his mouth.

"Did you see how Ari signs his work?" he said.

"Gil deSeaver," Stef said. "That's awesome."

A bit of silence. The two men let go hands.

"Kind of makes me want to change my name back," Jav said.

"So do it."

"I don't know. Two name changes in a career is a lot."

"If John Mellencamp can do it, you can," Geno said.

Jav laughed, glancing in the rearview mirror. "Good point."

Stef was checking his phone. "Oh boy, dude," he said. "You're trending on Twitter."

"I am?"

"You and Rog." Stef turned his phone and Jav gave a quick glance.

"I can't... Read it to me."

Geno unbuckled and hitched forward to read over Stef's shoulder.

OMG, @gilrafael and @thetreehouseguy spotted at #Newpaltz art show. Underwear just exploded. BTW, anyone else know GR was gay?

Attached to the tweet was a blurry but unmistakable picture of Jav and Stef, standing in the gallery. Their hands clasped behind Stef's back. Roger stood at their side, arms crossed, his expression thoughtful.

"She totally outed you," Stef said. "Us, rather."

Jav shrugged.

"It's not cool taking someone's picture secretly like that," Geno said. "In my biased opinion, obviously."

"No, it isn't," Stef said.

"She didn't even get my good side," Jav said.

Stef barked a single laugh. "That's your best side, Landes." Then he glanced over his shoulder at Geno. "Buckle up, junior."

"MAIL CALL," JUAN SAID, rattling knuckles on Geno's door. He held a small, flat package.

"For me?" Geno said, getting up.

"None other."

The return address read *A. Seaver* in New Paltz.

"No way," Geno said under his breath, already knowing what was in it. He slit the taped flaps and cleared away balls of newspaper. Cut through bubble wrap and brown paper, then the little square canvas with the red house was in his hands.

"Dude," he said. "Oh man..."

A small card was tucked in the back of the frame. *Aaron Seaver* with a phone number and email. A note crammed onto the back in small handwriting:

> *Geno,*
>
> *It was great meeting and talking to you. I've been thinking a lot about your henhouse story. To the point where I want to give this to you. I feel like art and stories are meant to be shared and when one bumps into another the way ours did... I almost didn't hang that painting in the exhibition. I had a blank spot on the wall that bugged me so I grabbed that canvas to fill it.*
>
> *Some things are meant to happen and call me nuts, but it just seems like this piece is supposed to be yours.*
>
> *I come to the city a lot to visit my dad and Jav so maybe I'll see you around.*
>
> *Take care,*
>
> *Ari*

Watching the Birds Move

In March Stef went to a week-long psychology conference at GWU. It was the first time they'd been separated since they started dating.

It didn't go very well.

"Dude, this *sucks*," Jav said. "And it's only Tuesday."

Stef laughed, while his bones moped. He was unprepared for this. He knew he'd miss the guy but he didn't know he'd miss him to the point it *hurt*. It was almost embarrassing. The more he told himself to knock it off and deal with it, to man up, for fuck's sake, it was just a week...the more it sucked. He felt lopsided. As if he'd gone deaf in one ear.

"I seem to have gotten used to you, Landes," he understated.

"Honestly, I thought I was going to enjoy the solitude," Jav said. "Be an unwashed, unshaven hermit for a week, eating while standing over the sink. I keep looking for you. And Roman's glaring at me all the time, like he thinks I buried you somewhere."

A bit of mournful silence curled over the phone line.

"Oh well," Jav said. "It is what it is."

"I'll be home soon," Stef said. There was nothing else for it.

It was a good conference. The lectures were superb, the workshops excellent. The time away was well-spent, it just seemed to drag on painfully. Turning every corner to bump into a brick wall spray painted with *I miss you*.

God, what if something happened to him? Stef thought, alone and wide-awake in his hotel bed. Then he had to fight like hell to get the fuck away from that thought.

Friday finally came but of course, Fate had to be a cunt about it, and delay Stef's train leaving Union Station. Then it had to cause some kind of trouble on the tracks that made them sit for an hour and a half in the middle of Maryland. Stef thought about abandoning ship and hitchhiking home, he was that desperate. At last though, he was at Penn Station. Rather than gamble the subway for three stops and risk getting trapped in a tunnel, he walked ten blocks downtown and risked getting hit by a cab.

Better odds, he thought.

Fitting his key into the door at Cushman Row, he felt like a soldier returned from war. The apartment was dark and sleepy. Roman gave a single yip and came jingling over to him, panting and licking and turning circles inside Stef's arms.

"Hey bud," Stef whispered. "Yeah, I missed you too. I'm home. Shh. Go back to sleep. Go on. Go to bed."

He heeled off his shoes, put his jacket over the back of the couch. Moved on socked feet to the bedroom. The little lamp on his corner altar threw a circle of light on the ceiling. Jav was asleep, the covers pulled up high, just the top of his crown visible.

Stef could smell him already.

He sat on the edge of the bed and put a hand on Jav's back. "Hey, you."

Jav made a small noise.

Slowly Stef peeled the edge of the comforter down from Jav's head. He leaned and softly bit Jav's ear. "I'm home."

"Mm." Jav's eyes stayed closed but the corners lifted. Stef kissed the radiating smile lines as his hand moved the covers down more. As Jav's bare shoulders were revealed, Stef drew a slow breath in, his heart beginning to race and his eyes narrowing.

The skin on Jav's back was filled with tattooed blobs of yellow and black and white.

Stef leaned closer, fingertips hovering but not touching. From Jav's right shoulder blade, in a diagonal under Trueblood's coordinates and across his spine, little inked birds swooped and flew and perched. One, two...four...six goldfinches in all.

"Oh man." Stef's mouth formed the words without a sound as he stared at the charm of finches on Jav's back.

"This for me?" he whispered, as finally his fingers touched.

"For me," Jav said. "So I don't miss you so damn much next time you go away. You like?"

"I love."

"Get in here."

Stef pulled off his clothes and slid into the warm cave of the bed. Jav was hot as an engine and hard like iron, wrapping arms and legs around Stef and pulling him in tight. "Missed you bad," he said against Stef's face.

Stef's hands couldn't get enough. His mouth couldn't get enough. He pulled free and rolled Jav down on his stomach. Enough light came from the corner lamp to make the goldfinches visible. Stef ran his tongue along them, gently licking the healing skin, kissing each bird.

"You don't know what it means to me," he said, his forehead pressed to the small of Jav's back.

"Yeah, I do."

Stef lay down again, now pulling Jav's heavy heat on top of him.

"Got another surprise for you," Jav said, sucking on Stef's neck.

"What?" He tilted his chin back, crazed, wanting Jav to mark him.

"You'll see."

"No, what?"

"You'll see. You'll find it." He was kissing Stef then. A kiss for the ages. A kiss that tore him slowly in half, made him want to whimper like a baby, moan like a whore, cry like a widower. His hands clutched in Jav's hair, slid down his back and curved around, pulling him in tight. Wanting to be one with that hot, hard energy.

His hands slid up the crack of Jav's ass, gently working in. His mouth pulled away from Jav's kiss as his fingers found a hard edge. The silicone base of a...

"You're wearing a plug?" he whispered.

Jav gently bit Stef's bottom lip. "Surprise."

"How long you had it in?"

"All night."

"Holy shit."

"Yeah." The wicked word breathed into Stef's mouth. "Thing's been rubbing me for hours now. I'm so fucking ready for your cock."

The covers exploded open as Stef rolled over onto Jav, pinning him down. They kissed like tigers, teeth and tongues, devouring. Stef eased the plug out and tossed it, then Jav reached for the top drawer. His slippery hands slid along Stef, then along himself. "Come on. Come here."

It happened so quick. Stef sunk in easy. It was like *nothing*. Past the initial resistance, a tiny pause where both of them took a breath. And then one slow magnificent slide until he was balls-deep in Jav, his hips right up against him, his chest laid out on Jav's beating heart.

"God, man."

"You don't know," Jav said, gasping.

"Tell me."

"I was out of my mind tonight, waiting for you to get home. This whole week. Feeling like an arm was missing. I couldn't stand not being able to touch you. I *needed* it so bad."

"I'm home." Stef pulled his hips back and carefully pushed in again. He could feel a wall torn down, a barrier broken and a fuck no longer given. "I'm home now."

"Feel good?" Jav whispered. "Tell me."

"So tight and hot." Stef rubbed his forehead along Jav's temple. "There's nothing like it. Nothing feels like this."

"You can go harder."

"You sure?"

"Try."

He carefully pulled out. "Turn over for me."

He fell forward on his hands and slid his cock back into Jav's ass. Balanced and braced on his arms, he ran his mouth up Jav's spine. Closed it around the nape of Jav's neck and gently bit as he moved further in. Jav's fingers curled down in the sheets and a moan popped out of his chest.

"All right?" Stef whispered, licking along the path of the goldfinches.

"Mm."

"I love watching the birds move on your back."

"That's why I put them there. *God...*"

"Hurt?"

"No, it's just intense."

"Spread your legs more," Stef whispered. "Let me in deep."

"God..."

"Let me fuck you." Stef leaned on Jav's wrists, moving in and out of him. "Let go and just take me."

Jav was arched and open like a strung bow, ready to fire. "Put it in me," he said, raw and exposed. "Everything you got, Finch, give it to me."

Stef pulled his lover's wrists down, held them behind his back and buried himself over and over in the heat. Jav's name, over and over in his mouth, huffing out with every exhale, morphing from *Jav* into *have, have, I have you now, you are mine and I have you...*

Jav yanked himself free from Stef's grip, planted palms and his knees in the mattress and rocked back onto Stef, fucking him. His fingers closed around Stef's wrist and guided that hand to his cock.

"Come," he said hoarsely. "Come now and take me with you. Do it."

Matching the rhythm of his thrusts, Stef stroked Jav over the edge and leaped after, his open mouth against the goldfinches. "I love you," he whispered, crossing forearms over Jav's collarbones.

Jav's head fell back, lolling on Stef's shoulder. "I love you so much."

"Jav, you're..."

"I know," Jav gasped. "I know..."

"You're everything," Stef whispered, rocking the two of them on their knees. "You are everything, everything, everything to me..."

WORDS MATTER

Jav drove up to New Paltz to take Ari out to dinner for his birthday.

"Think you'll marry Stef?" Ari asked, as they drove back to campus.

Jav smiled. "Would you be all right with that?"

"Me?" Ari laughed. "Why does what I think matter?"

"Because it does."

The moment curled between them, strange and touching. Each Gil deSoto realizing the other's opinion meant something.

"Anyway," Jav said. "I'm still trying not to trip on 'boyfriend.'"

Ari's lips twisted. "Well, neither of you are boys."

"Not age-wise."

"How do you like to refer to him?"

"Slave."

"C'mon."

Jav exhaled. "Boyfriend's too adolescent. Lover is fine in private but sounds affected and pretentious in conversation. I like partner. It has a two-ness sound to it. It captures the together thing. Me and him. Going along. Friends first and foremost." He shrugged. "I'm a writer. Words matter."

"No, partner's cool. That's what I use. When I talk about Stef, I mean. I say 'my uncle's partner.'"

Better than my uncle's nephew, Jav thought.

"Anyway," Ari said. "I'll be there."

"Where?"

"There. If you marry him, I'll be there. And if you don't marry him, I'll still be there."

Don't fucking cry, Jav thought. *Don't you fucking ruin this by crying, you sentimental sap.*

"Thanks, sobrino," he said aloud, pleased that his voice stayed steady.

A bit of silence.

"Just don't be screwing in front of my dog, okay?" Ari said.

The car wobbled in its lane as Jav burst out laughing and smacked the back of his hand against Ari's shoulder. "Shut up."

"I'm *just* saying," Ari said, whacking him back. "He's young and very impressionable. Holy shit, T, look at you *blushing*."

"Shut up," Jav said again, his face flaming.

"Since you're already embarrassed, I'll remind you to practice safe sex. A different condom every time, remember?"

"Karma's such a bitch," Jav muttered.

"I just don't want anything happening to you."

"Like what?"

"I don't know. AIDS or something."

Another eye-rolling *shut up* was on Jav's tongue, but he bit it back, peeking underneath Ari's joking to see what was really going on. Hearing the echo of a lament sobbed into his shoulder, not all that long ago.

I can't take losing anything else, T.

"You don't have to worry," he said. "We're tested, we're monogamous and we're very careful. I'll be around a good long while to give you shit. Okay?"

"'Kay."

A quarter mile went by in silence.

"How is it?" Ari said.

"What?"

Ari's hand made a little circle. "The sex."

"You really want to know?"

"No. Kind of. I'm curious. But no, I don't... I don't know why I even said it. Never mind. It was stupid."

"A bit of life advice from a whore? Think before you speak."

Ari groaned and slouched down in his seat. "I *said* I was sorry about that."

THREE THINGS

LEANING AGAINST THE BRICK PARAPET, snug between Jav's knees. A cold beer in hand, fireworks above, the air soft on his skin. Stef sank into the moment, humble and grateful and amazed at what life could be.

Jav's hand slid through Stef's hair, fingers folding and pulling a little bit. His mouth nuzzled at Stef's temple. His breath exhaled at Stef's ear. His thighs drew in, cradling Stef tighter.

"I'm getting a hard-on for you," he whispered.

"Good." Stef leaned back against Jav's chest, smiling. He felt the party's eyes turned in their direction. Some gazes curious, others loving. He'd never been happier in his life.

Jav's forearm slid across Stef's collarbones as his mouth closed around the top of Stef's ear. "Want you so bad."

"Oh?"

"Yeah." Jav's tongue lightly touched Stef's neck, just for a second. "Want to make you see a different kind of fireworks."

Stef gazed up at the sky, lolling under the soft caress of Jav's hand and the harder stroke of his words. He slid his free hand into his front pocket, casually arranging his growing erection.

"Come on," Jav whispered, breath warm on Stef's earlobe. "Let me take you home and fuck you."

Stef's chest swelled thick. "Right now?"

"I can't wait," Jav said. "I want to feel your heartbeat on my cock."

Heat swarmed Stef's face. Burning red, he gulped back laughter. "Jesus..."

"Come on." Jav's voice like ice cream melting on Stef's skin, hoarse with desire.

Stef leaned and looked up at his lover. A hundred sparkling colors in his eyes. Smile glistening with lust. "I'm getting the feeling you like me."

Jav's hand slid along Stef's jaw, then he kissed him. "I love you like hell, Finch."

"Damn, Landes. I've never seen you like this."

"You're the only one who's seen me like this."

"Get a room," someone yelled.

Jav didn't blink or blush, didn't break his gaze. "Come home," he said. "Come home and see more of me like this."

Stef smiled, shaking his head. He'd never been so turned on his life. So electric and alive and happy. He could've grabbed a chunk of the sky and crunched down on it like an apple, juice running down his chin.

To hoots and catcalls they waved goodbye and left. It took them ten minutes to get down the rooftop stairwell, stopping to kiss and grind on every other tread. Stef practically swallowed Jav's tongue in the elevator. It cost a monumental effort not to rip their pants open in the back of the cab. They were drooling by the time they got to Cushman Row, unbuckling and unzipping as they stampeded down the stairs. Stef was sure he'd be face-down over the kitchen counter before the door closed, but Jav found some last shreds of patience to lead him into the bedroom.

"Now," he breathed, getting Stef up against the wall. "Where were we?"

"Something about your cock and my heartbeat." Stef wrapped his arms around Jav's neck and pulled their open mouths together. "Unless you were just sweet talking me?"

"Dude, I'm gonna fuck you so slow," Jav whispered. "You won't come until tomorrow."

"No, don't. Need it tonight." He nearly whimpered as Jav pushed his pants down.

"Listen to you," Jav said. His voice soft. His hand rough. He kissed deep, then held his palm by Stef's mouth. "Wet it down for me."

Stef worked up some spit and slicked up Jav's hand.

"Take your pants off," Jav said, closing up Stef's cock in his wet hand.

His other hand tugged at Stef's shirt. "This off, too. Want you naked."

Stef pulled at his collar, heeled off his sneakers and kicked his jeans away. "I love when you tell me what you want."

"Three things I want." Jav's kiss turned tender, softly pulling Stef's mouth apart. "Just be mine forever."

"I'll do that yesterday."

"Take my clothes off."

Stef stripped him down in thirty seconds, shoes pegged against the baseboards, phone and wallet thudding onto the rug and spare change scattering across the floor. "What's three?"

"Let me fuck you all night."

"Done."

Jav drew Stef off the wall and pushed him toward the bed.

It started wild and got outrageous. Things came spilling out of them, raw and torrid, the air hissing with filth. One minute Stef toyed with ideas of soap and mouths and teaching lessons. The next he was the one being taught, flipped over and pummeled onto his hands and knees. Jav nudged him apart, pressed up against him and pushed slowly inside. Slow like he was intent on waiting until morning to breach it.

"Fucking tease," Stef said, gasping.

"You love it."

"I'll get you for this, you bastard."

"Shh... I love watching you open for me." Jav's lubed thumbs stroked around the delicate ring, easing it further apart, getting it to relax and stretch.

"Fuck me or I will kill you," Stef said. Or tried to say. It was sexy in his head but came out as babble on his tongue.

Jav was having no such issues. As he moved a millimeter further, he fucking *purred*. "There. I love when it gives way."

Stef bit down on his lip. *I am going to lose. My fucking. Mind.*

"God, look at that tight ass open for me."

"Put it in," Stef said, incoherent now. "Put it in me. Jesus fuck, *please*, Jav..."

"Shh." His hand curled around the back of Stef's neck and pushed his head toward the pillow. Face down. Ass up. Mouth open and knuckles white.

"Hold still," Jav said.

Not moving, Stef considered all options, including crying. "You're killing me."

"Shh. Just let me do this." His hand held Stef's head and he sank in more. Pressed down and pushed deep. Slow. Slower than death. Stef's fingertips curled into the sheets. His throat dissolved and he groaned his lungs empty as Jav filled him up to his eyes.

"So tight, baby," Jav whispered. "So fucking hot and tight in your ass. It's unreal."

Then he stretched out along Stef's back, nudging their bent knees straight. "Lie down," he said. "All the way down." His mouth closed on Stef's nape and his hands twined with Stef's. "Hold still, honey."

Honey was sweet on Stef's skin. Dripping and dabbling in ribbons down his back and all at once the room was clean and bright and pure. His mouth scrupulous with truth. His heart immaculate.

"God," he whispered against Jav's wrist. "What are you *doing* to me?"

"Nothing." Breath like warm velvet between his shoulder blades, followed by the drag of Jav's tongue. "Everything."

"Don't ever stop."

Jav trembled, his next exhale choppy and anxious. "You know I love you, right?"

"I know."

"Even when I fuck you hard and say raw shit like that. You know I love you more than anything in the world."

"I never doubt it. It all feels the same to me. It all feels like love."

A long, breathless moment, then Jav inhaled sharp through his nose. "Shit..."

"Hey." Stef curled a hand back to hold Jav's head on his shoulder. "There's no crying in fucking."

"I'm not crying." Jav laughed softly, then sniffed again. "You always *do* this to me."

"I love it. You can only fuck me like this because you love me. I know." He pushed up against Jav's weight a little. "I need to turn over," he said. "I need to face you. Let me up."

Jav carefully withdrew and moved back on his knees. He applied the last of the lube and tossed the empty bottle aside. Their third in a month.

"Now come here," Stef said, reaching up. "Get back in here."

Jav pressed in, all the way in, sliding along Stef's chest and burying his face in Stef's neck. "It's so much."

"I know," Stef whispered. "Just be in it, Jav. Love me and fuck me. There's no fucking difference. I trust you with my life." Stef held his brow against Jav's. "And you don't scare me."

Jav closed his teeth on Stef's bottom lip and slowly let go.

"Can't be too much," Stef said, "because it's never enough. Come on now. Show me. I love when you're raw. I love when you're sweet. I love when you talk dirty and I love when you cry. I love all of it."

Jav held his head tight and kissed him, tongue dipping and sliding and curling. His hips made long, slow thrusts now. Slick and slippery. Grinding deep at the top then easing back to the tip, holding the ring at its trembling peak.

"So fucking tight," Jav said. "Better than any pussy I had in my life, I swear." He slid forward again, then back, the length of him dragging within, making the air bump out of Stef's lungs in a stuttering cry.

"Feel good?" Jav whispered.

"God, I never had it so good."

Propped over Stef, Jav's eyes seemed to harden. "You ever gonna let anyone else fuck you like this?"

"No way. Never."

"Who do you belong to?"

"You."

"Who will you always belong to?"

"You. I'm fucking yours."

Jav kissed his mouth inside-out. "Want to make you come."

"Keep doing this, then," Stef said. "Keep talking to me. Keep kissing me and fucking me."

Jav took Stef's hand, licked the palm and slipped it between their bodies. "Jerk yourself off," he said. "Come with me."

He leaned hard. One hand on Stef's shoulder, the other pinning Stef's wrist, he fucked Stef clear through the bed down into the earth, while Stef stroked himself off and over, straight up into the sky.

"Right there, Jav," he said in a hiss. "There, there, right *there*, Jesus

146

fuck don't stop..."

White crackled in his peripheral like a lightning strike. Then he went dark. The master switch shut down for a pinprick of blackened silence.

I've been fucked senseless.

The circuit panel flicked back on and the world poured into his eyes, ears, nose, skin and mouth. Quintuple sensory overload.

"God," Jav cried, his head thrown back.

Stef bucked and sputtered while Jav thrust and cursed. They toppled in a tangle of sweaty limbs, gasping and groaning, trying to kiss but barely able to pant in each other's mouths. Jav's voice twisted around Stef's name, something between a laughing sob and a sighed moan.

"Shh," Stef said, his hands pressing on Jav's back. "Come down now. Come down." The electric pleasure crackled away, leaving the ache behind.

"Holy fuck," Jav said.

"I know. Hold still. Don't move anymore."

"You all right?"

"I'm fantastic but you need to get out now. Nice and easy."

Jav got off the bed, took a few stumbling steps and then paused with a hand on the dresser. "Whoa. Head rush."

"You okay?"

"Got up too fast."

"Careful." He lay sprawled in the bedclothes, pulse pounding at his temples. Jav had fucked the shit out of him. His rump burned and his hips howled. He'd be hurting tomorrow and thinking it *seemed* a good idea at the time...

He'd never been happier in his life.

STONES

In Maplewood Cemetery, Javier Landes sat cross-legged on the grass in front of his father's gravestone. He didn't acknowledge the stones of his uncles. Only gave the briefest glance to his cousin's marker. He had unfinished business there, but today was about him and Rafael.

From the inside pocket of his jacket he drew out a lottery ticket. He tucked it between the stone and the flower arrangement.

"Conocí a alguien, Papi," he said softly.

I met someone.

At Beth David Memorial Park, Geronimo Caan placed rocks on his parents' headstones. He'd painted a red hen on Analisa's, and written the word "kindness" beneath. He put a little hunchback on Nathan's, and wrote "sanctuary."

Last he drew a rock from his pocket, painted with a single star. It took him a few minutes to set it on his brother's grave. A few minutes more to open his hand and leave it there.

"Nos," he said inside his mouth, letting no sound escape.

He turned to go, then turned back to tell his family something.

"I met someone."

AT GUELISTEN VILLAGE CEMETERY, Roger Lark sat on a bench before his parents' headstone. They'd died together, suddenly and tragically in a car accident. Roger and his sisters had consoled themselves with the knowledge that one parent would never have to live without the other. They left together. They'd be together forever. Faithful for all the years left in time.

Roger rested his elbows on his knees, fingers clasped and thumbs tapping.

"Dad, I met someone," he said.

IN BARON HIRSCH CEMETERY, Stavroula Kalo knelt before a small marker stone, flat in the earth.

JACOBS
1997
Dear little one

It was a baby boy's remains beneath the rock. He would've been named Sam. Stavroula rendered the body to the earth but kept the name. The dream of another little boy she could name Sam kept her alive and hopeful.

"I met someone," she said, tracing the chiseled letters.

"PONY?"

"Hey Dad," Steffen Finch said. "Can you hear me?"

"I can hear you fine," Marcus said. "Where are you?"

"I'm on the Queensboro Bridge."

"You are? What brings you back to the old neighborhood?"

"Nothing. I just like this bridge. How are you?"

"Good, good. Can't complain. How are things with you?"

"Not bad," Stef said, leaning elbows on the railing and staring at the olive-green depths of the East River. "I met someone..."

THANK YOU

IF YOU ENJOYED *Tales from Cushman Row*, I'd love to hear about it. Please consider leaving a review on the sales platform of your choice (Amazon, Goodreads, iBooks, B&N, etc). Honest reviews are the tip jar of independent authors and each and every one is treasured.

You can read more of my little stories at suannelaqueurwrites.com. Stop by Suanne Laqueur, Author on Facebook or tweet me at @Suannelqr.

All feels welcome. And I always have coffee.

ABOUT THE AUTHOR

A FORMER PROFESSIONAL DANCER AND TEACHER, Suanne Laqueur went from choreographing music to choreographing words. Her work has been described as "Therapy Fiction," "Emotionally Intelligent Romance" and "Contemporary Train Wreck."

Laqueur's novel *An Exaltation of Larks* was the Grand Prize winner in the 2017 Writer's Digest Awards. Her debut novel *The Man I Love* won a gold medal in the 2015 Readers' Favorite Book Awards and was named Best Debut in the Feathered Quill Book Awards. Her follow-up novel, *Give Me Your Answer True*, was also a gold medal winner at the 2016 RFBA.

Laqueur graduated from Alfred University with a double major in dance and theater. She taught at the Carol Bierman School of Ballet Arts in Croton-on-Hudson for ten years. An avid reader, cook and gardener, she started her blog EatsReadsThinks in 2010.

Suanne lives in Westchester County, New York with her husband and two children.

ALSO BY SUANNE LAQUEUR

THE FISH TALES
The Man I Love
Give Me Your Answer True
Here to Stay
The Ones That Got Away

VENERY
An Exaltation of Larks
A Charm of Finches
Tales from Cushman Row